good deed rain

Gilead Baum had not been around for very long,
but his mantra made a ripple in the pond.

This is
the author's 61st book.
Others include:
Another Life, Island Air,
Field of Cabbages,
Lexington Brown &
the Pond Projector,
and many more…

AMERICAN MANTRA

AMERICAN MANTRA © 2023
Allen Frost, Good Deed Rain
Bellingham, Washington
ISBN: 978-1-0880-2960-2

Writing: Allen Frost
Cover Production: Priya Shalauta
Illustrations: Robert Huck
Apple: TFK!
Credits:
Paul Valery, *The Art of Poetry*, Vintage Books, NY, 1961.
John Keel, *The Eighth Tower*, Saturday Review Press, New York, 1975.
Jack Spicer, *The House that Jack Built: The Collected Lectures of Jack Spicer*, Edited by Peter Gizzi, Wesleyan University Press, 1998.
Richard Hugo, *The Triggering Town, Lectures and Essays on Poetry and Writing*, W.W. Norton & Company, New York, 1979.
Fritz Leiber, *Our Lady of Darkness*, Berkeley Publishing Corp., NY, 1977.
Horror Hotel, Shepperton Studios, 1961.

For J.Genius who created Baum's famous poem.

AMERICAN MANTRA

Allen Frost

Good Deed Rain ◊ Bellingham, Washington ◊ 2023

they can be clearly distinguished from the majority of people by the ease with which they are extremely moved by things that move no one else

—Paul Valery

Out there in the night thousands of sincere people are even now spending all their spare time laboriously writing down the long, involved messages they are receiving from that mysterious phonograph in the sky, unaware that millions before them have received the very same information and wasted their lives trying to find a publisher or just an audience.

—John Keel

"I don't really think that the dream world is any more real than the real world is…It seems to me that there's a world in between them that goes into both of them."

—Jack Spicer

One problem for modern poets is the wholesale changes in what we see—the tearing down of buildings, the development of new housing, the accelerated rate of loss of all things that can serve as visual checkpoints and sources of stability… With the accumulated losses of knowns, the imagination is faced with the problem of preserving the world…

—Richard Hugo

"I think all modern cities, especially the crass, newly built, highly industrial ones, should have ghosts. They are a civilizing influence."

—Fritz Leiber

"Who's to say where imagination ends and truth begins."

—*Horror Hotel*

INTRODUCTION

It's hard to believe I'm getting close to retirement. The long wished-for Xanadu of every working fool! To get by all these long 9-hour days, a regular feature, as eagerly anticipated as Jack Benny's shows, are the emails I send and receive from J.Genius. He's in the same boat as me, but now he has a job a half hour down the road. Years ago, we became instant friends when he started work with me in the library. One Halloween he came to work dressed as Ed Wood. I was wearing a cardboard Capitalist cuckoo clock, the poor bird with an arrow through his heart. We made quite a pair. One of our constant email ingredients is making up curious names, with occupations for them. Constance DuCanne was one. And that's how Gordon Mono was born too. It seemed ordained they be given more to do. So here they are.

Johnston Dracula is a favorite character of Mr. Genius, who first met him on the pages of a little sewn book I made in 2000. J.G suggested Johnston's reappearance in Chapter 29, where he falls in love with a moth.

The illustrations are by Robert Huck (star of *The Robert Huck Museum*) who was still around in 1955. The anonymous haunted cover photos of old Fairhaven are from a set of three prints someone gave me in a folder years ago. You should see what Fairhaven looks like now!

Originally, I was writing this novel where each chapter ended with directions to turn to another page. In keeping with time-travel, these chapters would have the ability to move—you could potentially find yourself going back and forth in time. But it didn't seem necessary, as with any book, you're free to read it however you want. The controls have been turned over to you!

—A.F in early April 2023

The CHAPTERS

1

The PLEDGE of ALLEGIANCE

It wasn't always like this. There was a time these streets knew his poetry. The gutters and spouts tapped with the rain, car tires sighed on the wet paving, another train rumbled its slow way, a night like this had an atmosphere. He could always be walking in 1955 when the sun went down. West Chestnut was waiting for him in the night like it always did. The trees were a little bigger and stretched to touch over the road, some of them were gone and replaced by younger ones, no more than brooms tied in place. He would be a welcome sight at The Crooked Stairs, but there wouldn't be poetry tonight.

He got all the way to the blue neon light of the café then Gordon Mono turned around. He was getting closer, it's true, like a rock in space he was caught in an orbit that every month drew him nearer and he was almost to the first stair that led down into the cellar. If he could only tell himself it was alright to do it all over again. That was the hard part. It felt like the weight of Saturn letting go as he crossed the street, heading for to the emptiness of outer space. Behind him, he heard the door of the coffeehouse open and shut. Funny, he thought, if someone calls my name I might go back.

The silhouette that just left Crook's was Gilead Baum. The door let out the sound of music and voices in the crowd. Gilead felt like a star as he walked away. This must be what it feels like to be a poet, he thought. Folded in his jacket pocket was his poem. He only had one poem but every time he read it he could see how it affected everyone. Maybe they could tell the words were from another dimension. His poem worked on them like a magic spell. They asked him for more. But that he couldn't do, all he had was one. To be honest, Gilead Baum had a secret. He wasn't really a poet. He didn't want anyone to know he was a time-traveler. He returned to 1955 looking for a legend. The dreams of the future depended on a poet, alive at this time, in this very city, and unbeknownst to Gilead, his prey was only half a block away. His quest could have been resolved with an easy "hello!" and a wave. He could have told Gordon Mono who he was and why he was here, for the Holy Grail. Oh, if only it was that simple. Too bad it never is…not when it comes to poetry.

Gilead had been searching for Gordon Mono for two weeks. He had been anywhere he thought a poet might go, to every coffeehouse, library, fire escape landing, bookshop aisles, the Aurora Bridge at sunset.

What he didn't expect was that Gordon Mono didn't want to be found. That realization was slow to dawn on Gilead. In his future, poetry was a national treasure. For crying out loud, Gilead almost shouted when he thought about it, there ought to be a statue of Gordon Mono in town! Gilead couldn't understand it. Where he came from, Emily Dickinson was on the dollar bill. She was everywhere, used for a cup of coffee, turned into change for a parking meter, left on tables as tips. He laughed when he saw George Washington taking her place in the past, it looked counterfeit. There may have been a sort of evolution at work, poetry was still underground like seeds, murmured or yelled like spells, it hadn't yet made it onto the dollar bill.

Oh well, Gilead had his work cut out for him. He only had two more days to contact Gordon Mono. If only he caught up with that shadow on West Chestnut.

By then Gilead had reached the end of the block where his time-machine waited for him in the dark. He reached into his pocket and got the key. Without it he would be marooned in this time. That wasn't a fate he thought about yet. The key recognized the whorl of his thumb and the door clicked open. He sat down behind the wheel. He looked forward to the day he would return with Mono's stack of poetry on the seat next to him. With it transplanted safely in the future, his life could go on. Yes, it was only a matter of time. And meanwhile, Gilead would string that one poem of his through town as bait.

The poem was generated by a computer in the future. People relied on computers for everything. His office computer composed it just before he left. Gilead thought he would only need one poem to direct him to Gordon Mono. But after two weeks of reading it in coffeehouses and cafés he wasn't any closer, or so he felt.

He ought to have it memorized by now. That wouldn't be difficult. But Gilead kept it pressed in his shirt pocket until it was ready to be unfolded and read. Gilead smiled and looked at the world back there reflected in the car mirror. Behind him he could still see that neon glimmer of The Crooked Stairs. He imagined his words still floating like moths in the air. He put a hand on his shirt pocket the way a kid will do when reciting the Pledge of Allegiance and he felt the power of that poem. Words can do that. He was happy. It was a good night. "Nailed it," he said with a smile.

ROBERTS
CO.
GRA
CO

2.
1955 AWAITS

It started in the future. Gilead Baum waited in the parking lot for his time-travel machine to roll from the garage. Over the years, parking lots haven't changed a great deal. A sharpened, electric barrier surrounded the paving. You couldn't just walk off the street and get a time machine, once you were through the forcefield, users had to register and fill out forms and once they got their transport, they were carefully monitored driving away. Also, there was the cost, far beyond what a reporter like Gilead Baum could pay. The *Herald* was picking up the tab. Their employees were regulars at Tic Toc Travel. Last 4th of July, Gilead interviewed Thomas Jefferson. He won a Peabody Award for that.

Baum was at Tic Toc Travel because his boss Lewton Wen had another big story in mind. Bigger than Thomas Jefferson. An adventure that would make frontpage news. Gilead was going to 1955.

America, seventy years ago. Imagine.

He kicked a bit of gravel and it almost made it to the ghostly fence. He heard something happen behind the garage door. 1955 was a chrome wave of cars, the Chevrolet Bel-Air, the Thunderbird, Chryslers and Packards, the Plymouth Belvedere, DeSotos, Cadillacs and Ford trucks. He was excited to see the car they were giving him. Power steering and automatic transmission. What a change from the horse he rode to find Jefferson. This time he was going back in style.

Before the garage could reveal his gleaming machine, the office door swung open at the end of the lot and a cardboard robot approached Gilead. It wobbled, thrown off balance by the enormous clipboard it carried.

"More paperwork?" Gilead groaned.

"Affirmative," the robot answered.

"I thought we were done."

The robot stopped before him and held out the clipboard. Its spindly arms bent under the weight. "It will not take long. Would you care for some music?" It had a quarter slot. Who knows what it would play.

"No." Gilead took hold of the chained pen.

"Do I have to sign all these?" The stack was thick as a novel.

"We only need your signature on the blue copies, the ones on top. The rest will be delivered to the *Herald* finance department for their approval."

"Okay, okay." Gilead was signing the last document when the garage door began to clank open. "Ahah!"

A thin grin of chrome emerged from the garage, a wallflower smile, not the wide, million dollar grill he hoped for. The engine sputtered nervously. More of it slowly appeared. A mustard yellow car the years had worn down like a shoe. It bore no resemblance to the glamour of the 1950s. Was it even from that time? Maybe. Maybe it was built in some bleak Iron Curtain country where the sun could only be seen through a telescope, if it wasn't caught and arrested for trying to shine.

The car stopped. Its engine clucked a few times like a chicken settling. The door cracked open and the driver got out. "Get some grease on those hinges," she told the mechanic watching from the garage.

Gilead hesitated. How was this car going to fly through time?

"What a beauty," the robot whistled.

"Are you kidding me?" Gilead circled the car. "What is it?" he asked the driver.

"A Maverick."

"I never heard of it."

"Ford made 32,000 of them in 1973. It was state of the art for its time. You should be impressed—and this is the only one left—the last of its kind."

"Wait—1973?"

She nodded and she stepped aside to let the mechanic get to the door hinges with his grease-gun.

Gilead persisted, "But I'm going back to 1955, not 1973. I can't show up driving this."

She seemed to take offence, "I don't see why not."

"It's a twenty-year difference! That car's not going to fool anyone."

"Sure it will," she promised, "You'll fit right in."

Gilead looked at the shadowy depths of the garage. "You don't have anything closer to 1955?"

"We're not a museum. I couldn't find the exact year but makes and models change so little down the years."

"No Cadillacs?"

She laughed and looked over her shoulder, "You hear that, Hank? He wants a Cadillac."

The mechanic scoffed. He wiped the excess grease off the door. Hank prided himself on his work, even if he sometimes missed things, it was the overall effect of what it could do, how it could carry you miraculously to another world. He told her, "The car is ready."

Rejoyce said thanks and she handed the keys to Gilead. "1955 awaits."

3.
CONSTANCE DuCANNE

Gilead was about to drive away. He rented a room in a big boarding house. Up on the third floor. It was a tall house, there was one more floor above him. The steep roof slanted like a gothic tower. Painted in red letters across the indigo face of the house above the door was: Wallace Stevens Poetry House. What poor poet could resist that sign? Gilead felt sure he would run into Gordon Mono but so far he hadn't. It seemed like the perfect lodging for that elusive poet. He put the car into reverse and as he looked into the rearview mirror, he saw a girl running towards him, waving her arm for him to wait. Her breath puffed in the cold.

He cut the engine and leaned over the passenger seat to roll down the window.

Her voice carried ahead of her, "Hey Galahad! Wait! Galahad!" little clouds in the dark.

"Gilead," he corrected her.

She leaned on the windowsill. "Right," she clapped her forehead like an actress forgetting her line. "Gilead."

"What's the matter? Do they want me to read another poem?"

"What? No." Then she thought of something, "Do you *have* another poem?"

He shook his head. He insisted there was nothing more to say, but was there? Did he need to do something about that? Maybe that was just all he had, maybe that was all he needed to get through. "What's this about, Constance?"

"I didn't get a chance to ask if you found Gordon Mono yet."

"I wanted to ask you that too." They were both obsessed with Gordon Mono.

Constance DuCanne wanted to find him just as badly. She had her own recording studio in her apartment. Her records could be found in the coffeehouse jukeboxes or played in the soda-shop. Her most recent 45 single was titled "The Starlings Are Making A Racket Outside." Three minutes of the birds on the rooftop. Twenty seconds in, you could hear a streetcar go past. She viewed that recording as poetry. To get Gordon Mono had been her dream since she started hearing rumors of him. "I haven't seen him, have you?"

"No."

The small silhouette far ahead of them was Gordon Mono turning the corner onto West Chestnut Street. They had no idea.

Constance asked, "No clues even?"

He shook his head. "I'm giving up for the day."

"It's weird," she said. "He just dropped out of sight."

"I'm beginning to think that's true."

"Okay…"

Gilead snapped his fingers. "Oh, say, I was wondering about our record. I have to leave town in a couple days. Do you know when it will be ready?"

"Soon. I think we've got enough now." Constance still leaned on the chromeless rim of the open window. She didn't pay much attention to cars but she could tell there was something odd about this one. He kept it a secret, if anyone pressed him on it, he would say it was from another country far away. Sometimes he said Transylvania. It was a car from the future, but nobody was much impressed—the car was quite plain compared to their silvery atomic chariots. If anyone pondered the truth, it would only be to wonder, "Is this the best the future has in store?" She pointed at the odd snowglobe set in the dashboard. "What is that?"

All Gilead needed was one mistake and his cover would be blown, and he could never return to 1955. Gordon Mono would stay lost in time. Usually, he kept the dashboard partially hidden by his leather jacket. It was a cold night though and he had foolishly worn it to Crook's. Anybody on the sidewalk could have looked through the window and seen the controls. "Oh that?" He had to think quick, but he could only lie the truth, "This is a time-machine." He grinned a little and hoped to hear her laugh. When she did it was a big relief, and it gave him the chance to put the gear back in reverse. "I'll see you, Constance."

"Yeah, at Serenade. Seven o'clock, okay?"

He saluted. She let go of the car. The Maverick drove from her. Around the corner, it drove past Gordon Mono making a big shadow on the wall of a warehouse.

4.
GORDON MONO'S DREAM JOB

Gordon Mono thought about The Crooked Stairs café. Part of him was tempted, the urge had been there a while, but he didn't have time to stop, he had a job to do, he was gathering dreams.

1955 was The Cold War. Underneath all the Hollywood Age, there were dark war-rooms with pins in maps on the wall and cigarette smoke clouding above. Atomic bombs blew up in the desert and the wind blew across the whole country. There was radiation in every town. And the military minds had a new idea for a new kind of weapon. First the A-Bomb, then the H-Bomb and now there was the D-Bomb. Believe it or not, Gordon Mono didn't know he was part of anything sinister, he was just gathering dreams the way someone would catch butterflies.

So how did he get his strange job? You might say it fell on him. At the end of last autumn, he had been walking home from reading at Alphabets. The sidewalk was lit here and there by a streetlamp. On the corner of Girard, he stopped for the traffic light. A gust of wind blew some litter around his feet. He was right below a dream-box perched on a loose rung of the telephone pole. It rattled and fell off. It hit him as he stood there, just about to take a step into the street. When he woke up, he was in St. Joseph's hospital.

Two men in dark suits and fedoras were waiting for him.

Gordon stirred. His arm was wrapped like a mummy. They explained how responsible they felt for him, it was their machine that hit him. But they stressed it was no ordinary machine, it was part of a top-secret invention that could ensure the safety of the entire free world. (In the 1950s, Americans believed that story). And if word got out about what happened, if the *Herald* got involved and people started talking, it would mean the end of their research. Governments are supposed to care for their citizens, they're supposed to know what's best and care for their country. Maybe this experiment really would save the world. It was his patriotic duty to stay quiet about what happened.

Besides, they made sure the hospital bill was settled and they even gave Gordon a paying job.

He carried a collector pole and a bucket. It wasn't a bad job for a poet. It got him outdoors, he could wander, he had quiet to think, and he could write between stops. The pay was unlike anything he ever made before. He could use it to print his book. There was an ad in the back of a pulp magazine, PUBLISH YOUR OWN BOOK. Once he got the money together, he would send it to them. There was something else too—what if he could start his own café? That had been his dream for years, to open the Shakespeare Café.

A memorized map was in his mind. He followed its red line every time the sun went down. He had plenty of stops, looping all around the town, stopping at streetlamps and telephone poles, for the boxes like crab-traps flown up into the sky to catch dreams. Every night he was back at that corner on Girard Street. The dream-box had been repaired and secured surely to the telephone pole. He would raise the dream-collector stick and retrieve whatever dreams were in it. Then he lowered the stick and emptied the dreams into the bucket on the sidewalk.

When it was dawn and he was done, he would wait for the ice-cream truck. A perfect disguise. A little white ice-cream truck that rang a bell only dogs could hear. It would take the dreams and he could go back to the Leopold and sleep.

Of course, Gordon Mono wondered what all these dreams were being collected for. The D-Bomb was still in the testing stage, a top-secret mirage. You wouldn't read about it in the *Herald*, not until it was done. If every dream could be analyzed, some overwhelming fear common to everyone could be turned into a frequency and detonated in the air. With an entire town paralyzed by fear, an army could march right in. That was the theory anyway.

At the end of his imaginary map, when the bucket was full, Mono stopped at a phonebooth. He called the number he always called and pretty soon the little ice-cream truck arrived. It wasn't playing its Pied Piper music—that would have been funny though, with kids in pajamas chasing after it. Mono gave the driver the bucket. Gordon couldn't see it being emptied, but in a moment it was returned to him lighter. That was the last he would see of those dreams. He watched the truck drive away. He didn't know the dreams were on their way to being poured into a wall of blinking lights, switches and spinning reels.

5.
In the FUTURE

Before Tic Toc Travel let Gilead drive away, Hank attached a tracker, a curious rounded snow-globe device, near the radio. Rejoyce said, "We usually hide these below the dashboard, but we want it to remind you, your time is limited, you're from the future and you can't stay long. Normally we don't tell people about the tracker, but we're having some trouble with the traveler before you." Rejoyce made sure Gilead understood his whereabouts would be carefully monitored. And he was not to remove the tracker or tamper with it or else. "You could get lost in time," she warned.

The robot had Gilead sign for the tracker too. Examining that page on the clipboard, it observed, "Your penmanship is quite…unique."

Gilead really didn't like that robot. Whoever installed its personality must have been having a bad day at the factory. They probably dropped it on the floor like Igor. So what if my writing looks like a crabbed snarl, he thought, that's because I'm a poet. He had to think of himself that way. Where he was going, that's what he would be. He checked again for the poem in his suit pocket and was satisfied. He was ready to go. He turned the key and started the car. He didn't have to drive far. The car stayed in the same physical place, out the windows, the same city would melt and twist and unform, into a very different looking town. All he had to do was press a button.

The future spun from sight and he was in 1955. Just like that.

A sunny blue sky.

The Maverick sat in a field—an odd field—he was in the grassy backrow of a drive-in movie parking lot. Ahead of him and on either side were rows of white painted speaker poles planted at car window height. There was one beside his window, the speaker staring in at him, a grilled face and a single round volume control. Honestly, its features resembled the robot with the clipboard.

Gilead rolled the window down. In the future, this site was paved and clamoring with the sound of Tic Toc Travel's garage, but now this was just a spring day on the edge of town, peaceful until nightfall when the white screen at the far end of the lot would be shining with James Dean and watched by a hundred cars.

He supposed it wouldn't be hard to find a phonebooth in town. They used to be everywhere. He could leaf through the phonebook and look up Gordon Mono. Gilead moved the car into gear and bumped slowly over the field. The exit was off to the left, past the big Moonlite Drive-In sign that read: *The Phantom from 10,000 Leagues* and *It Came from Beneath the Sea*. As he steered with one hand, his free hand pretended to dial the phone and here's what he said, "Hello, is this Mr. Mono? Good day, sir. My name is Baum. I've traveled quite a way to see you. I'm very interested in your poetry."

6

DuCANNE RECORDING STUDIO

Constance watched the weird car leave. It melted like a pat of butter around the corner, then she started walking again. She was carrying a heavy suitcase. Inside it was a reel-to-reel recorder. She had been taping Gilead Baum for a week, going everywhere he read his poem from the aqueduct to the waterfront, at The Green Marilyn Coffeehouse, The Cat Racket, Loathsome (the club where after every act, the MC's catchphrase was, "Do you loathe it?"), The Existential ? (where the cook made meals blindfolded), So and So's, Sorry Charlie's, The Doghouse, down to the stone steps leading into Crooks.

There were enough performances of him reading his poem to fill a 45 with songs, but she needed something to be music in the background for three minutes each side. The music she was looking for arrived quite by accident. By chance, she left the microphone pressed while walking home and she captured the surrounding night. When she discovered that, she was delighted. Things that happen that way are meant to be.

Luckily she didn't live much further than a couple of jukebox sides.

Her apartment was around the back of the house on the ground floor. A porch with big windows looked down the hill to the black sea. The light was on inside making all the panes glow warmly. A stand of moonflowers bloomed below.

It was her dream to get Gordon Mono on tape.

She had to settle for Gilead Baum and his one poem, but she figured it would be good practice to press a single for him. DuCanne Recording Studio was still pretty new, the painted sign on the door looked wet in the porch light, but she had been busy at work, gathering every sound she could think of in this small 1955 town. She wanted the memory of this fleeting moment in time to stay alive.

Pushed in the seam of the door was a note. That wasn't unusual. Yesterday there was a request for a radio jingle. If she turned around and looked back towards town, she would see the red light on that tall radio tower on top of the Leopold. Just think, someday her sounds could be transmitted down the coast, and maybe to radios as far away as California on a clear night. But that wasn't what she was in this for.

She unfolded the paper and read, *Mizz D—the record is Smashville! Can we get some more? We play at Alphabets on Friday night. You should come! Your friends in The Paper Mill.* That made her smile. The Paper Mill's single was "Comet Shake." Rock and Roll was in the air. It was like knowing the circus train was coming, you could feel the change as it neared and the shockwaves poured ahead. All these kids were lighting up guitars and drums with electricity, going right into the ground. She tucked the note into her pocket. A letter from The Paper Mill was worth holding onto. One day it would be framed and hanging on a museum wall.

She turned the handle and went in. The lamplight on the porch table made it seem like an aquarium the way the windows held shadows and reflections. Her studio was off to left. That's where she lifted the suitcase onto a console and set it flat. That's when she noticed the machine had been recording the whole way home. That's how she suddenly discovered the background sound for Gilead Baum's poetry single.

It wouldn't take her long to get a mix. She could already hear it in her mind, she just had to piece it together. She crossed the room and started the record press. After a while it would warm up and she could stamp some vinyl.

7.
A JUKEBOX REVOLUTION

He sounded like a square in a 1950s Maryland suburb. But not when he was on record:

"The bus. A long cube of transit.
We all get in.
We're all going somewhere."

She remembered the way Gilead Baum stared at the audience for a suspenseful twenty seconds after he read it. As if he was soberly daring them. It was the same poem but each time he recited from a new café, store, or even before a tree in the backyard, it sounded different. She ran the sounds through the board and was quick to sew two sides together. Thinking of a title took her a few seconds. He never told her if it had a name. Wherever he was, he would just stand there and say three lines of a poem that changed but stayed the same. She treated it like a song. "Transit" was side A, "Going Somewhere" was Side B.

She was pleased with Gilead's record, listening to it a few times on the record player. The way the town walked along in the background really worked to give those three lines momentum, as if you were truly on a bus going somewhere. She put a couple new records in her bag along with some more Paper Mill sides. Shell's Diner had a jukebox in the back corner, near where the cook could hear it while he stirred around the stovetop, five meals going at once. "Comet Shake" and "Transit" were about to be added to all the other 45s, Buddy Holly, The Platters, Howlin' Wolf, Patsy Cline. She made tracks for all the jukeboxes in town stocking them with DRS hits, like the one by a truckdriver from Memphis who stopped in one night and sang "Blue Moon."

That's what the jukebox was playing when Constance went into Shell's. The owner Michelle stood by the register and gave her a nod. Shell liked to keep an eye on her diner. You can imagine the sort of crowd they attracted at 4 A.M. A small factory town had nowhere else to go at that hour. There were three rail workers talking in a booth. A milkman finishing a cup of coffee. A man in black at the counter on a stool, hunched like a raven. Constance passed him and went to the cash register.

Shell said, "You got records?"

"A new one," Constance said. "Hot off the press."

"That's fine." Shell reached under the counter for the jukebox key hanging on a little hook. She also kept a blackjack there. Ever since Shell saw *The Wild One* at the Moonlite Drive-In, she could tell revolution was on the way and when it came, she was ready. While she fed the young and gave them a place and their music was on the juke, if trouble like Marlon Brando came crashing in, she wanted to stay in control. This was her place. It would play by her rules. "Here's the key, honey. What you got this time?"

"Something different," Constance said with a smile. She didn't know if the diner was ready, this little cast of characters at 4 A.M., the night owl crew from Northern Pacific, the milkman, the cook, Shell, and the shadowy figure at the counter, but they were about to find out.

"Blue Moon" was ending, crackling, as she opened the lid of the jukebox and put poetry in.

You could play it for a dime, three times for a quarter.

8.

MAKING NIGHT NEVER END

Constance walked back along the counter past the view into the kitchen and the cook looked out at her with a grin. "Play it again," he said. So she did. Then she played Side B, then Side A one more time. She had seen this reaction before with other records she made, it was like the people in this town were waiting for something new. They were ripe for it.

As she sat at the counter, the milkman stopped beside her and patted her shoulder on his way to the door. He told her, "That's the sound I hear every morning when I'm out on the streets delivering." Shell brought her a mug of coffee and showed her the dime pinched in her fingers that she was putting in the record machine for another play. "Transit" and "Going Somewhere" were going to be in the air a lot that day.

While Constance was adding some cream to her coffee, stirring it so it whirled like a little cyclone,

52

a voice rasped from the stool next to her. "What a splendid recording."

"Thank you," she said. It was the man wearing black. He was immersed in the color of night, nearly completely lost from view, topped by a charcoal fedora, his bony face mostly hidden by a wrapped scarf, eyes blinkered by dark lens glasses, only his long fingers extending from the heavy sleeves of his woolen coat. They held tightly to a sandwich, roast beef it looked like, so raw a red trickle crept down his thumb.

"It reminds me of many things," he slowly croaked. "Pleasures and pain, the frailty of life."

"Wow," she said. Here it is, she thought, my next project, this strange man cut from the cloth of midnight. If I can get him to talk for six minutes, that's another record.

They both listened for a moment as the record began its spell. Shell stood there at the machine and watched it spin.

He asked Constance, "I wonder if I may purchase that record from you."

"Really?" It was hard to imagine who this black cocoon beside her was. Maybe he was an advance man from Imperial Records sent out to scout for more talent? Maybe he was just one of those nocturnal creatures who know loneliness only too well. That seemed more likely to her. She sensed a wound that had been patched a hundred times. "I have another one in the car. I'll give it to you, my pleasure."

"Ohh, that would be delightful."

"I won't be long."

Side B started as she left her coffee cup—she heard her own footsteps on Mercer Street, recorded only hours ago but kept in a forever nighttime as long as "Going Somewhere" played. Maybe that was it, the appeal for the diner's shadow man, maybe it made the night never end.

She walked into the parking lot in front of Shell's. The milk truck shone like the moon. There were two other cars, counting her own. Her car was familiar around town, a 1935 sedan. A Studebaker Dictator. Even in 1955 they were rare, a twenty-year-old car looked almost desperate by now. It was something George Raft would drive in a gangster picture, sneering as he crashed it into marble.

Constance opened the passenger door and got her bag off the seat, found a record, shut the door—there was no need to lock it, nobody did—and waded back into the pond of light coming from the diner windows.

A robin chirped in the silhouette of a tree.

The sun was just breaking through the leaves to the east.

She yawned. She hadn't slept at all, she felt like a haunted deep-sea diver. Yes, the world seemed watery and she pushed against it up the steps to the door.

Gilead Baum was nearly done. Fats Domino was standing by, the next one in the jukebox, hands on a piano, ready to break the trance.

"Where's that man who was sitting here?" Constance asked Shell. He abandoned his spot at the counter, his plate and fork, not even a message written on the napkin in crabbed lettering.

"He left."

"Left already? He was just here. I didn't see him go."

"He's in the supply closet," Shell said. Constance was confused. Shell could read that, plain as day and she explained, "His name's Johnston. Johnston Dracula. He's a vampire." She reached over the counter and took the plate with the gummed sandwich. "When the sun comes up, he has to hide."

"I have a record for him," Constance said. Her words sounded run aground. "He wanted it."

"Oh, you can slide it under the door." Shell wiped the red formica where the plate had been then pointed at the kitchen wall. "Come around the counter, honey."

Constance quickly obeyed. This was weird... There were a lot of weird things about 1955, but vampires wandering around...Did he have a record player in among the mops and brooms and boxes of detergent? If she opened the door would the very fact that day had arrived turn him into a skeleton?

9.
The DREAM COLLECTOR

It was dawn. Gordon Mono often found that dreams didn't really get good until the sun started to rise. Maybe sleepers were intuitively aware the day was starting and suddenly knew there wasn't much time left for dreaming. Those last dreams padded the last dream-box like parrot feathers in a nest. It was a good catch. His bucket was full. He turned them in and went home to the Leopold and shut his curtains—there was a reason to keep those curtains open at night, he had a moonflower growing in a clay pot next to the window. It needed starlight and the bright glow of the moon.

He rested the pole next to his bed and put the bucket on his desk beside a poem he was working on. Then he lay back on the bed and shut his eyes on the day. He was still in time to join the weekend sleepers. On Saturdays people like sleeping in if they can, their alarm clocks watch them wide-eyed while 6 AM rolls past. Saturdays were best for catching dreams. So he left the traps in the air to give day all the time it needed before he pulled them down at night. This job was turning him into a vampire. A water pipe in the wall made a racket. Cars went by on the street below, a pigeon cooed on the window ledge, the radiator hissed. It didn't take him long to fall asleep. It took even less time for him to wake.

He opened his eyes. It could have been dawn or sundown. Did he sleep at all? Maybe a nightmare. Or was it a daymare? Whatever mare it was, night or day, the dream vanished from him quickly as a horse runs over the next hill. A hole in the curtain let a beam of orange dying sunlight reach across the gloom. He sat up and put his hand on it. It filled his palm. A patch of warm sun. He wondered if you could catch that sun in the collector like one of the dreams and examine the contents to see what the day had been. Daytime was a different world, foreign as another planet. He let the light slide off his hand. Soon the sun would go behind the factory hurrying away from the falling night.

As he got out of bed, he disturbed the dream-collector pole which slid towards him along the mattress. He caught it. In its glass vial on top, something washed. A dream. One he hadn't poured into the ice-cream truck. He knew enough about dreams to know it was a nightmare. It clouded and billowed like ash. The storm was streaked with thin bloodred snaps like lightning. That was his bad dream alright. The pole's ON switch was never turned to OFF. With the pole lying beside his pillow while he slept, it had taken his dreams.

Oh no, he stirred. And right away, I have to let it go. He didn't want to see his dream used in whatever game they were playing. All this time and he had never released the collector, they were for the little ice-cream truck. Not this one though.

When Gordon Mono unscrewed the lid, the dream boiled out, making a big inkblot in the air. He didn't have long to marvel or fear it. With all the predatory speed of a panther, the nightmare rushed him. The attack was so sudden and unexpected, it wrapped around him completely and fell with him backwards, through the last coppery ray of the setting sun.

Unlike most hunters, Gilead Baum wasn't exactly sure what Gordon Mono looked like. Gilead wasn't even certain where Mono lived, this town was his Loch Ness, foggy, cragged, gloomy and deep. Somewhere in it, Mono had to lurk. Of course Baum had no idea that every day he was searching, Gordon Mono was way up high in the Leopold building, sound asleep. He might as well have been in Kathmandu.

Gilead's wallet held a blurry black and white photo of the poet, the only reference he had. It wasn't much to go on. The 1955 parade starred a lot of people who looked like him. Gilead kept thinking he saw Mono everywhere he went. He even asked an old man at the grocery if he liked poetry. That was a strange thing to ask someone in the soup aisle.

But that was how he met Constance DuCanne. She overheard Gilead stammer, "I'm sorry, it's just that I've been looking everywhere for a poet who lives in our town." The old man who bore only a slight resemblance to Mono's blur speedily wheeled his cart away, as Constance stepped in.

"Who are you looking for?" she asked. "What poet I mean."

Gilead viewed the pretty young woman and launched right in, "Gordon Mono," and was practically shocked by the electricity that lit up behind her cat-eye glasses.

"I'm looking for him too!" she said. "He's the most!"

If it was a movie, there would have been an orchestra digging in at just this moment, the camera would've whirled around them as the music played. The scene could have been two catastrophe survivors meeting by chance years later upon a Paris street. But there were rows of cans on either side, boxes of rice and lentils in need of water. It was a strange place to find someone with the same goal as you. They chattered back and forth excitedly while a teenage boy with a broom swept past, saying nothing but sharing a quick glance. He dreamed of something like this happening to him.

Gilead's wallet also held her telephone number.

Constance told him to call her immediately with any Gordon Mono news. And he gave her the number of the phone at Wallace Stevens' house. Whenever it rang in that wooden hall, he would hope it was her.

How much did he let on? Did he tell her he was from the future and the future depended on poetry? No, of course not. And when she told him about DuCanne Recording Studio and how it was her dream to record Gordon Mono, she stretched her arms wide as a butterfly collector hoping to net a *Hamadryas amphinome*. Did she say any more? No. They both had their secrets.

11.
BIRD SCHOOL

The Paper Mill was four boys in school, first period homeroom. One afternoon not long ago, Constance overheard their band in a car garage one lucky day. It was like music from another planet. She asked if they wanted a record made. DRS#19, "Comet Shake" and "Homework Blues." She was lucky she discovered them before anyone else—talk about being in the right place at the right time. She often carried a suitcase wherever she went, always ready to tape anything that might be of interest, always hoping it would be Gordon Mono. Like Buddy Holly would say in a year, "That'll be the day."

Morning happened fast, the sky was turning a pale blue, she was driving past houses that stirred. An ice-cream truck drove by. Its appearance didn't seem unusual anymore, she had seen it before, at dawn and also dusk. She supposed it was just making the rounds.

She parked in the high school lot between two jalopies. When the big V-6 rattled into silence, she could hear birds, there must have been a hundred of them singing in the trees surrounding the playground. Her car didn't have a radio, she didn't need one with this kind of music. Her suitcase was on the bench seat next to her, she was quick to get the microphone, unspooling the wire, setting it on the narrow dashboard, pressing the red button and getting lost in listening. After six minutes she pressed STOP. "Bird School" would make a great jukebox wonder.

The winter day was going like a bicycle. The branches were rattling with the breeze. She opened the car and got out carrying her handbag and the suitcase. Before she left the car, she pressed RECORD. It took 56 seconds to go up the steps and enter. The front door made as much noise as a castle's complete with a Frankenstein creak and bang as it closed. Her shoes clicked on the linoleum fourteen seconds before she stopped at the office.

"Good morning," said a woman at the desk. She had a microphone too, the morning's announcement, a pile of paperwork and a telephone. A daisy flower wilted in a pitcher.

"Hello, my name is Constance DuCanne. I have a present I'd like to leave for The Paper Mill. Is that possible?"

"Oh those boys!" the receptionist said. "Aren't they something!"

Constance wasn't sure what that meant or how to answer. She got the stack of records anyway while the receptionist explained, "They're the best thing to happen to my garage. I used to have rats in there. Not anymore!"

"Well…" Constance motioned the records towards her.

"Say! You could sell these at Woolworths! Put them next to the rattraps and they'll sell like hotcakes."

"Okay. Could you give these to them?"

"Of course, miss. You can put them here on my desk."

Constance thanked her and gave a little wave as she turned and left the office. She was seven or so steps away from the doorway clicking again on the waxy linoleum when she heard the speakers come to life. "Attention students in The Paper Mill. Please report to the main office." Like two hundred pigeons, from behind every door you could hear the classrooms go, "oooooooooooh!"

12.

DAYLIGHT

There wasn't much to room 481. A painting on one wall of an old sailing ship, a hundred miles from land. A radiator prone to tapping out Morse code. A kitchen in one corner, a sink and a hotplate. A coffee percolator. A desk with a typewriter. A stack of paper. A moonflower on the sill of the only window. A bed from 1938. And on the floor next to the collection pole, like a blind man who had died, was the body of Gordon Mono.

Someone in the hall knocked on the door. "Mr. Mono! You in there?"

The second barrage of knocking woke Gordon up. "What is it?" he croaked.

"Mr. Mono, you got someone on the phone wants to talk to you."

The dream that had circled him and held him down was gone, disappeared as they do, and the details were already forgotten. Gordon shook his head. "Okay…I'm on the way."

Whoever it was, the neighbor across the hall, or someone on either side next door, they left Mono's door and were gone by the time he stumbled into the hall. He wasn't used to sleeping on the floor, that escaped dream had knocked him for a loop. Where did it go anyway? Did it leave this way too? Out the door, down the elevator, into the day?

The telephone clung to the wallpaper, the receiver hanging from it towards the floor. There were only a few people who knew his phone number. He guessed who it must be. "Hello?"

It was the dayshift dream-collector, Clark.

Gordon didn't see Clark often. Clark's dayshift was mostly old folks asleep in chairs, or kids taking naps—their dreams were fantastic cartoon things, bright colors jumbling, as opposed to the pale papery ones found at the retirement center, blurring next to the sandstone bluff on the Parkway.

This won't be good, Gordon thought as he listened to the voice.

"I called in sick today. Can you take my rounds?"

"I just got done!"

"I know. I'm sorry. Listen Mono, I owe you one."

"I was sleeping. I think I was…What time is it?"

"Come on, Mono." begged Clark, adding a cough.

Oh, what's the use, he thought, he didn't want to go back to sleep, that bad dream on the loose was enough to make him say, "Okay." Before he left his room, he checked around the desk and under the bed. He knew it was only a dream, but it could still be hiding somewhere.

Daylight made a different world. It was the same downtown he was walking in, the same route he took into the next neighborhood when he started his job at night, but nothing was the same. Have you ever really noticed an oak tree in the sunlight? The sidewalk sparkled with stars of mica, a million of them dusting the cement to the next curb. He stopped so he could write something in a notebook.

He turned the page and wrote a little more.

When he shut the notebook, put it away and looked up, he saw a person crumpled on the next corner. Gordon could tell what happened, the same thing happened to him not so long ago. Twelve feet off the street, the dream-box got loose and fell off the telephone pole, smack onto some poor soul underneath. Didn't the company care enough to tighten all the bolts? Or maybe this was how they hired people—knock them out and promise them a great job. Gordon hurried towards the accident. Next to the broken dream-box, cracked like a miner's lantern, was the body of Gilead Baum.

13.
MEET GORDON MONO

Rewind time just a little bit.

Constance only wanted to sleep for a couple hours, she didn't want to lose the whole day, so she set her alarm before shutting her eyes. A block away moving parallel with her, walking under the trees on Girard Street, Gilead Baum was starting the day's search for Gordon Mono. He paused on the street corner. The town went everywhere. At this point he was thinking he needed a miracle. If two people looking for Mono couldn't turn anything up, what were their chances?

He began every search with the question: if I was a poet, where would I be, what would I be doing?

Then a dream-box fell off the lamppost and narrowly missed Gilead as it crashed on the sidewalk, releasing a swarm of dreams that stormed out in a bee-like skirl and stung the nearest person, some poor time-traveler from another century.

Gordon Mono was almost there, he recognized the silky haze that covered that patch of cement like a veil, he knew what it looked like when a dream got loose.

A sparrow could fly from Gerard Street over the row of houses and their backyards and land in the tree outside Constance DuCanne's window. If it looked in, it would see the blankets and her face on the pillow, with her eyes closed and know she was in the dreamworld.

Gilead Baum was with her. He was watching her dream like a movie as she moved in the future he came from. He saw familiar buildings and the sky was the right color and all of a sudden they were at Tic Toc Travel. Rejoyce told Constance, "You need to come back. You're already overdue."

"I can't," said Constance, "I'm not done. I promise I'll come back as soon as I get that record made."

"You're breaking the contract," the robot told her, lifting the heavy clipboard.

Seeing that robot again, Gilead wanted to walk up to it and kick its can, but all he could do was watch.

And look who else was there to scold her—

Lewton Wen, "You had your time to find Mono. You failed. We sent someone else to take your place."

"What? Who?"

"You won't have any trouble finding him." Lewton didn't have to name him.

Gilead watched Constance turn to look at him and they noticed each other for the first time in the dream.

"I want that Studebaker," Hank said sternly. "Now."

Then Gilead was opening his eyes, seeing blue sky and Gordon Mono was erasing the dream with wild swipes at the air, waving a stick around. "What happened?"

"You fell. I think you fainted. Is your arm hurt?"

Gilead held his left arm, his wrist, moving it was painful.

"Let me help you stand." And then the man offered the scarf he wore. "Here, you can use this, let me tie it around, there, like a sling. Hopefully it's only a sprain. Put some ice on it soon as you can."

Gilead promised he would.

There was nothing more Gordon could do, he couldn't leave all the dream-boxes filled with those luxurious dreams of people sleeping in. He picked up the broken remains of what looked like a birdhouse and carried it with the bucket. As he left, he tapped the pavement ahead of him with what looked like a staff.

Gilead rubbed his eyes. What happened? He didn't faint. He got pulled into a dream…What was it? Constance was in it. The memory was melting like wax. He couldn't hold on to it…So he stopped worrying about it. His arm did feel better tied with the plaid scarf.

At the end of the block, lit by the morning sun, the man with the staff was reaching up the next lamppost.

That's how Gilead Baum finally met Gordon Mono, not even knowing it was him, and all he got from it was his arm in a sling.

14.
ALMOST BEAUTIFUL

"Where is she?" Lewton Wen barked. "Did we lose her again?"

"She must have woken up," one of the technicians answered.

"Yeah," the other technician agreed. The screen in front of her was blank, all the needles and dials had died. "Dream's over."

"Well, I hope we got through to her. I hope Constance remembers what we said." Lewton crossed his arms. His shoe ground a scritching bit of gravel into the paving.

The man next to him offered, "We all heard her say she would return as soon as she got the record. The subconscious mind doesn't lie."

"Nertz!" Lewton growled, "I didn't ask for your flim-flam. If she doesn't get back here soon, I'm making a run."

"Don't forget the Studebaker," said Hank.

Rejoyce asked, "What about Baum? He's been there two weeks. Neither one of them is getting the job done."

"I know! I don't get it. What's so hard about recording some pop-nutty poet!"

Everyone around the *Herald* editor slammed into silence. Even the bird on the rain gutter got quiet. On the other side of the fence, Tate Street was frozen. Amherst under snow. "Sorry," he begged, "I didn't mean that." Wen had gone meek as a scarecrow. No surprise, the future of their society depended on a poem, a few good words to break their spell.

What happened? What was wrong with the future? Well, I suppose it won't hurt to tell.

Since 1955 the D-Bomb had been carefully stored under the desert until well into the 21st Century when it was unboxed and brought to the Smithsonian Museum. People flowed around the glass cube and stared at the bomb. It resembled a puffer fish with all its spikes pointing out. It was almost beautiful, but it was a bomb, designed to go off, and that's what it did, the most powerful D-Bomb ever constructed. After a moment's panic, all that seemed to have happened was the bomb had broken in half. Nobody noticed anything wrong until they tried to sleep.

15

MISSING GORDON MONO

Gordon Mono went down the steps of The Crooked Stairs for the first time in a hundred years. That's what it felt like, but it also felt like he never left. He opened the old green painted door and walked into the same old place. Two people playing chess, a table with a crumpled newspaper, teapot and cups, the woodstove against the wall, the counter, the pie dome, the kitchen, the urns and all the other details rushing in. He noticed the poster with his name on it and looked away.

He leaned the pole and set the bucket down and told the girl across the counter, "Good morning."

"Afternoon," she said, correcting him.

He nodded, "You're right," and shrugged helplessly, "I don't know where I am, I only know I need a coffee please." As if coffee could take the place of sleep.

Upstairs at a table beside the window he sat with his dream-collector gear and coffee and watched the window movie. It turned out he needed three more refills before he felt ready to return to the streets. He wondered if Clark took breaks during the dayshift. So many shops, so many people out and about, Gordon was enjoying the town come to life. On the nightshift not much was open, there was a 24-hour diner and a gas station that served a paper cup full of tar. Some of that so-called coffee and he could make it to dawn. He saw a couple go past holding hands. A girl on a bicycle with a dog in the basket. A line of kids from the daycare, being led along the sidewalk, tied together like a string of geese. A streetcar rattling on the track, the birds heard through the transom. Gordon realized how much he missed the daylight and seeing everyone. By the time he finished his coffee, he decided he would tell the ice-cream truck driver he wanted to quit.

"This is it," he said as he gathered his gear and started for the stairs. Only a half hour went by before he needed another coffee at Serenade. Did it even do any good? The waitress made Martian eyes at him and that helped more.

When Constance DuCanne arrived there later, Marjorie said, "Oh!" as she set a cup for her on the counter. "You'll never guess who was here an hour ago."

Constance didn't have to guess—she could tell by the way Marjorie looked at her, it was obvious in her eyes—Constance didn't have to say the name, she talked about him every day.

Marjorie said, "You just missed him! Gordon Mono was here!"

Constance crumpled her fingers together and took a deep breath. It was okay, she calmed herself. It was destiny. He was somewhere ahead of her, only an hour away.

16.
SID and IMOGENE

In the Wallace Stevens Poetry House, three bachelors were making three different meals in the kitchen. The smell carried through the boarding house, three burning pans, oil hissing, fish, chili, and a hash made of Spam. The windows were open, anxious for breeze, at least they learned that much from experience. Gilead went past the kitchen with a glance, saw the cloud of smoke fluming about the stove, scuffed up the wooden stairs. The steps continued to a fourth floor, with an attic room higher still, but he left them and followed his hall. The key scratched at the lock and opened an unquiet door. There wasn't much to his room, a bed, some lanky furniture, a window framing a red-budded chestnut tree.

He had some time before the poetry reading tonight. He went to his bed and sat down on the uneven springs. A blue jay rasped behind the glass. It might want in, but it wouldn't find much of interest, this was the room of a man with only a short time.

Gilead let his fingers move along his sling, they played an invisible piano without hurting. A quick rub along his sleeve and he was pleased his arm was only faintly numb. The scarf had cured him perhaps. Were there healing properties to it, was the cloth run with papyrus strands and herbs picked along the River Nile? Is this what wrapped up a mummy going to the next world? He unwound the scarf, patted it onto the bedside table and put his wallet atop. He flexed his arm and he felt better, but something nagged at him. He opened his wallet and took out the picture of Gordon Mono. Yes, he noticed something in the coal gray photo he never paid attention to before. Gordon Mono was wearing a plaid scarf with his suit.

It was the same scarf that tied Gilead Baum's arm.

Then in a sudden flash, Gilead realized he had met Gordon Mono.

And he let him walk away!

What was Constance going to say when he told her? Gilead could see her grabbing his shoulders and shaking him, "Are you kidding me?" She would consider him a prize fool for letting that chance slip from them, but he had to call her. Maybe she would laugh. He got a dime off the dresser and headed for the door. Maybe she would forgive him if he let her wear Gordon Mono's scarf.

The savage kitchen smell crept along the wallpaper in the hallway, by now it had crawled throughout the house. It wasn't something that could be tamed in a circus, every night at this time it seeped and bristled and roamed until more windows went up to let it out. Gilead was used to it. He went right through it to the pay telephone and dropped a coin.

After a couple of rings, Constance answered. "DuCanne Recording Studios."

"Hi, it's me. Gilead."

"I was about to phone you!" She quickly rattled off where she had been and who had been seen in the café an hour before her. When Gilead told her his Gordon Mono story, she laughed at their absurdity and he laughed with her. It was the sort of thing you'd see on *Your Show of Shows* with Sid Caesar and Imogene Coca.

17.
BEFORE and AFTER

Gordon Mono waited for the ice-cream truck. It was nearly sunset. He was dead on his feet. There were few other times in his life he had gone without sleep for so long. He remembered walking with a girl all night, all around the town, looking at black windows and hooting like owls, resting some places on benches and she would lean against him then, with her hair for him to breathe, but they didn't want to sleep, they wanted to see the way the new blue light washed in and turned the streets to silver. It happened every day but how many people were watching? They wanted to be eternal, alive, and see the world the way it was before and after it stirred with robots and electric cars.

He saw the lights of the truck come shining like eyes catting up Magnolia Street with the other traffic. He picked up his bucket. It was still heavy. Who knew dreams carried that much weight? Well, Gordon and Clark did, they had callouses where they held the handle. As the truck pulled into the nearly deserted parking lot and stopped, Gordon suddenly wondered, who was going to empty the dream-boxes tonight? No amount of Crook's coffee could reanimate him and drag him through another shift. With the stagger of an old farm horse, he brought the bucket to the driver's window and lifted it.

The driver looked puzzled. "Where's Clark?"

"He called in sick. I covered his shift."

"First I heard of that." The driver took the bucket inside where it was out of sight and where Gordon guessed it was splashed into some big storage tank and vacuum sealed. "You tell headquarters?"

"No. How could I? I don't know anything about this organization. I don't even know your name."

"You're not supposed to," the driver said curtly. "This is a top-secret project."

"Right. That much I know."

The driver held the empty bucket through the window for Gordon. He let the bucket wag in his hand. "Then who's collecting dreams tonight?"

Gordon shrugged. "I can't. As a matter of fact,

I don't want to do this job anymore. I quit."

"You what?" The driver braced himself, frozen like the Emperor of Ice-Cream.

"You can keep the bucket. And the pole too. Here," Gordon pushed the collector stick over the window chrome. "Today I realized how much I like daylight. Now I have to go home and sleep. Tomorrow," he yawned, "I'm going to wake up where I belong, in the right world."

18.
SERENADE

"What if we see Gordon Mono tonight?" Constance bubbled. "I can tell it's going to happen soon, there's something in the air."

Marjorie liked talking about Gordon Mono with Constance. They bonded over it. There was an electric current whenever Constance got started on her favorite topic and it swept you up with it. Marjorie lit the candle on Constance's table. Serenade was transforming itself from a café on Lynn Street to a salon in Budapest.

Marjorie chirped, "Tell me, is that weirdo Gilead going to be here?" Everyone but Constance believed the rumor that Gilead was a government agent. He was older than most of the crowd, he dressed like Eisenhower, and his one and only poem seemed chiseled on the marble of an elementary school. No doubt about it, he was what the kids would like to say, a square. But they put up with him, they kept him on their radar, they didn't want to get on his bad side because who wanted what those suits like him dished out on North Korea.

"Marjorie! He's a poet."

"I know, *we're all on the bus together.*"

"That's right. Oh! That reminds me—" she reached into her bag and took out a stack of records. "Gee, I was so wrapped up in Gordon Mono, I forgot to tell Gilead about this."

"He has a record?" Marjorie looked at one.

"Yes, and won't he be surprised."

"Wow," Marjorie said, "Like Ray Charles."

"Well…"

"Does he sing and play guitar?"

"No. He recites his poem."

Marjorie looked stunned, "For a whole record? Both sides?"

"I put one in the jukebox at Shell's and they loved it."

That was as far as their conversation went, Serenade was gathering a crowd, Marjorie was a waitress and people were waiting for her. A girl played Chopin on the piano while the room filled, chairs, tables, the window ledge, the sidewalk outside.

19.
The KEY WEST REENACTMENT

He tapped the microphone and said, "Testing, testing." He didn't have to do that, it was working fine, but it quieted the room for what would come next. "Good evening, I'm Zale Figaro. I'm the manager of the Wallace Stevens Poetry House, a collective where artists gather and live. As most of you know, I am celebrating the life of the recently departed but never forgotten poet of our time, Wallace Stevens. Tonight, allow me to take you to Key West, Florida. The place, outside the Casa Marina hotel, where our hero trades blows with another literary giant, Ernest Hemingway. I will be playing both parts." He shut his eyes and whispered, "Follow me…back to 1936…" The girl who had been playing piano earlier sat beside him on the floor with a harmonium on the spread-out folds of her dress. A bellowed drone filled the room.

"So, you're that poet everyone's talking about?"

Zale blustered, with a shuffling, bent posture.

Then he turned and became Wallace Stevens, lithe and erudite. "Ernest Hemingway, I presume? The pleasure is mine. You're quite the poet yourself." He stuck out his hand for a shake.

Zale spun again and turned into Hemingway. "I don't want that delicate mitt! But if it's a fight you want, brother you got it!" With that, he swung a fist raggedly.

Wallace Stevens ducked and returned with a perfectly thrown right hook. He stared at the floor, "I'm sorry I had to do that, you made me though. Here…" he reached down, "Take my hand. But try anything unruly and I'll put you right back in that puddle."

Zale quickly dropped to the floor and summoned the wounded Hemingway. "Alright…I know when I'm licked…" As he took hold of Stevens' hand, he began to rise, just far enough to launch a kick.

With lightning speed Zale's Wallace Stevens caught that leg and flipped his assailant right back into the splash. "Not so fast, old man in the sea. No!—" he warned, raising his mighty fist again, "You stay in that pool. I can assure you I've never seen anyone land in such a spectacular fashion, especially into a large puddle of water in the street in front of a hotel. I hope you like that rainwater. I hope you find inspiration there, or at the very least I hope you've learned your lesson. It isn't all blood and gristle, life and death, that's not all there is. There is poetry in every blessed moment in between." Zale held that triumphant pose and waited frozen for the harmonium wheeze to die.

Someone began to clap and quickly the room filled with applause. Zale could breathe again. "Thank you, ladies and gentlemen," he bowed. "We'll take a five-minute break now. Thank you. Thank you very much."

As the audience began to move, chairs chirping on the floor, talking and a song from the piano again, Constance heard a voice near her ear.

"That was interesting."

"Gilead!" she cried, turning round to face him. "You're here!"

"I wouldn't miss this for the world," he answered.

"I have a present for you." She dug into her shoulder bag. "I made a record for you."

Gilead inhaled and held the gift like a bird at

rest on his hand. He didn't know what to say, it was a dream come true.

The star of the Key West reenactment interrupted whatever moment these two were lost in, "There, you see…" Zale dabbed at his forehead with a red kerchief. "You're like Wallace Stevens and Elsie Viola. There really *is* poetry in between."

20.
MONO in PRINT

In Gordon Mono's room is a manuscript. What was he going to do with all his poems? At first, he thought of the pigeons on the roof of the Leopold. He could take the elevator up there every early morning home from the job and each day he could tie poems to the birds before they were released. Eventually the poems would fall, in the air a hundred feet up, or in the park, below a bench, skittering on cement, or finding another rooftop where someone grew a garden. It was haphazard, randomly targeting the city, and he would be utterly lucky if anyone saw them, but it was his way of getting his words out into the world.

But then he thought of an even better idea— the newspaper.

Gordon Mono knew someone who worked at the *Herald*, a clerk with a desk, a lamp, two ashtrays, a typewriter and a telephone. Usually a paper cup of coffee from the vending machine made a ring on the pad he took notes in. People would call him and he'd put their message in the Classifieds. Garage sales, swap meets, church bazaars, For Rents, lost dogs, lonely hearts, jobs at the mill, used cars, weddings and obituaries, and scattered in here and there every week, Mono's poems. It was ingenious. Gordon Mono got his poems printed in the newspaper by listing them as classified ads! Those brittle poems on pulp newsprint were taped into a bound sketchbook he kept in the drawer under the moonflower by the window. This was the only evidence of his writing in print and who knows where it ended up. Gilead never did find it, but if anyone looks at the back pages of the microfilmed *Herald* from 1955, there they are, more than a hundred, hidden in plain sight.

21

The DOTTY MACK SHOW

All the lights of town around them made a kind of dew in the black night. The Maverick reflected in Woolworths' windows. A little Nash Metropolitan puttered from the curb after it.

Constance asked Gilead if she could turn the radio on. Her Studebaker didn't have a radio. She missed it, it was nice to have a little soundtrack as you drove. On top of the Leopold, way up at the end of the radio tower a red warning light blinked. She spun the simple plastic radio dial across bristling static, stations playing music or talking, until she found what she was looking for.

Gilead said, "Did you ever hear of Betty and Benny?"

"No."

"I was at Sig's Barbershop last week and I saw a photo of them on the wall. They were acrobats. In 1929 they spent 19 hours balancing on a wire on the Leopold tower. There were searchlights on them all night. They had to stay awake the whole time. One little slip like falling asleep and it was all over."

Constance wasn't really listening to him, she was listening to the radio, Thelonious Monk was playing 'Round Midnight.' She sighed, "People were doing amazing things back then."

"You have no idea—the future is even more amazing." He almost made a mistake and told her, he barely stopped himself before he said too much. She didn't notice though, her attention was on the music.

She said, "This is the pirate radio station."

"Pirates?"

"They don't have a license. They're breaking every known rule playing this kind of music." She laughed. "Isn't it great? Nobody knows who they are. They move like The Shadow from place to place, so they don't get caught. Each day, they transmit from another secret location. And guess what? Tomorrow, they want me to play some records. You know how I got directions?"

"They sent you a parrot?"

"I had to go to Safeway, to the aisle with the soup. I had to find the third can of corn chowder from the left of tomato. When I turned it over, I found a piece of paper, no bigger than a fortune cookie message."

He glanced at her, "That doesn't seem very smart to leave directions on a shelf in a grocery store. What if someone else got it?"

"Nobody buys corn chowder."

He thought about that. It's true he didn't know anyone who liked corn chowder. But somehow it remained. Even in the future you could get it. Whoever these devotees were, there were just enough of them to keep it in stock. Either that, or it was a common means for the underground to get their messages across.

"There's my house," Constance said, pointing across the dashboard at the silhouette in the trees. "Thanks for the ride."

"My pleasure. Thank you for the record. I can't believe it. I can't wait to hear it. There's a turntable in the common room, I'll play it as soon as I get back." Then he added, "As long as they're not watching *The Dotty Mack Show*."

The Maverick stopped in the driveway. The little dome light fuzzed to life as she opened the door and said goodnight.

22.
DREAM in MONO

Gordon Mono was in luck. When he fell asleep that evening, his dreams stayed where they were, they weren't drawn into the air and beehived into a streetcorner contraption on level with the wires. The mysterious dream operation was finished. The ice-cream truck disappeared. It was nearly spring. There would be another truck like it once summer appeared, but it would only carry popsicles, cones, and fudgesicles.

He was in a familiar dream city. It might have had something to do with reality, there were landmarks that almost made sense. He knew it from years of exploring—the stores, the houses, where all the buses were going   and he knew from experience if he walked down the stairs inside that building, he would find a gorilla. Ever since he was a child, he'd been filling the dreamworld with his imagination.

Where was he going? The landscape moved as

it does in a dream, like a rollercoaster.

The sky was filled with twirling things.

His winter dreams would be studied by the creators of the D-Bomb. Some poem he dreamed up was so important, time-travelers from the future would search for him. Was there a connection? Were his dreams poetry?

A telephone was ringing on the trunk of a tree. He answered it and heard a voice say, "I'm going to give you a mantra, ancient words, and I'd like you to repeat it back to me and if it's right, I'll say yes, and you don't ever say it again." Another poem that wouldn't be heard.

Then he was at a laundromat. It looked like the one he used, except some of the washing machines held aquarium fish. And there was a tiger wearing a bathrobe, waiting for his orange fur coat to finish its tumbling cycle. Across from the tiger sat a leopard in a blue robe, legs crossed in a chair, doing the same thing, waiting. It was reading a magazine. They took their coats out when they were ready. Still stripes and spots. Then they decided to switch.

"It's a little tight on you," said the leopard.

"No, it's fine," the tiger said. "And you look

good in stripes."

Gordon Mono held a poem big as a pillowcase. There was something wrong with the words. He handed it over the counter to be dry cleaned. He could see the steam press and more poems hanging from the conveyor track on the ceiling.

A woman took it from him, and gave him a ticket and said, "You can pick it up tomorrow."

He turned to leave.

The fish were swimming.

The tiger and leopard were switching coats again.

Funny, he thought. He didn't exactly know why. There was a joke in there, a joke that probably only made sense in a dreamland.

23.
DuCANNE DREAM STUDIO

He would be bigger than Elvis. She would be more than Colonel Parker. It was raining, but they were under the eaves outside. Gordon Mono spoke into the turning tapes, Constance held another microphone up to a window and recorded the high school jazz band practicing in the background. Her first record with him, *Mono in Mono* was only the beginning.

Gordon Mono was going to take over the world, they would go by bus to all the towns, by train to cities they had never seen. In New York City, they would be on TV. Steamships and airplanes would take them even further. London, Copenhagen, Cairo, Bombay. There were factories producing his merchandise. The Moonlite Drive-In would project his movies. He would live in a castle and float on a pool and when he died it would be front page of the *Herald*, Long Live the King, and for years afterward the tabloids would report he was still alive.

But also, Constance wouldn't forget Gilead Baum, who only had one thing to say, who mesmerized the early morning people at Shell's. She designed a toy bus that can recite his poem when the wheels are rolling across the floor.

24.
GILEAD'S DREAM

It wasn't Dotty Mack on the wooden TV in the Wallace Stevens Poetry House common room. Three boarders were sitting on the couch watching *The $64,000 Question.* Gilead couldn't play his record while the fate of that contest hung in the air like the cloud of cigarette smoke layering the ceiling. That took some getting used to for Gilead, everyone everywhere was smoking cigarettes. People left trails behind them like steamships. The three guys on the couch glanced at Gilead as he passed the kitchen doorway on his way upstairs. It wouldn't be polite to interrupt. He would come back down when the program was over and hope they were gone…unless they started watching *What's My Line?* Then forget it, he'd go to sleep and play the record in the morning.

At 10:30 P.M, Gilead carried his record to the landing. He could still hear the television.

It sounded like a Western, he heard a horse. A guitar was playing. So just like he was afraid would happen, he gave up and returned to his room, put the record on the nightstand and went to bed.

What a day…He thought about Gordon Mono—he finally discovered Mono was here. He thought about Constance DuCanne and the record. What would it sound like? Soon it would spin on the turntable. It would be on pirate radio tomorrow. Then he was asleep.

There might have been a few warmups, short scenes, as he sailed into a deeper sleep.

The lot around Tic Toc Travel surrounded Gilead, along with the people who worked there.

Rejoyce said, "You're in a dream, Mr. Baum. This is the only way we can reach you."

Gilead blurted, "I saw Gordon Mono! We met!"

"Really? Did you get a poem from him?"

"No," Gilead admitted, "But he gave me a scarf. Will that help?"

"Listen, Mr. Baum. You'll probably forget about this meeting, or think it's just another throwaway dream, but this is important. We're bringing you back tomorrow."

Behind her, Hank added, "Enough is enough."

Gilead told them he wasn't ready, he felt sure he was going to see Gordon Mono again very soon. He didn't want to leave. He didn't want everything to disappear, he never got to hear the record Constance made. He got himself so worked up he woke up. The room was quiet. No rattling waterpipe or radiator. When he turned over, the bed springs twisted and squealed. The green radium numbers on the clock dial glowed 3:17.

"I'll find Gordon Mono," he said.

He turned over again, setting the bed to undulation. His eyes were open, he didn't want to go back to sleep. He didn't want to leave 1955. The time he went back to 1780 to speak with Thomas Jefferson, he didn't feel this way. He couldn't sleep. Each time he looked at the clock, it just kept marching along. What if he went downstairs and listened to his poetry?

25.

The AMERICAN DREAM

We're not getting a quantum physics engineer to describe how the D-Bomb works. What would be the point? Besides, that information is still highly classified, we wouldn't want someone reading this to try and make one. I can explain some basics though. Over the winter of 1954 into 1955, day and night, the dreams of a papermill town in the Pacific Northwest were recorded. We can't precisely say what was discovered by feeding those dreams into the banks of a gigantic computer, or exactly how they were sifted through and condensed into a horrendous weapon, The Dream Bomb.

It may sound like hocus-pocus, but after the accident at the Smithsonian, when the antique bomb split in half and spilled out hollow nights, filling sleep with emptiness, the future had no more dreams.

All I can say is there's a cure constructed in such a way that it makes a perfect antidote to the effects of the D-Bomb. It will put people to sleep again, a sleep of dreams. There's a poem, the one Gilead Baum is after and Constance DuCanne is trying to record, that is said to be the only thing to break the spell of the D-Bomb. Don't worry if it doesn't make sense to us, we're not rocket scientists, suffice it to say the future put two people into time-machine cars and sent them a long way into the past. Constance was a recording engineer, Gilead was a proven, capable reporter. On paper, they should have been perfect, but Constance and Gilead weren't having much luck. That's the way the *Herald* saw it. And at the prices Tic Toc Travel charged, two spinning wheels getting nowhere were two too many.

26.
The SUN of the FUTURE

Gilead stayed where he was, in bed, tossing and turning for another hour until he fell back asleep.

He was at Tic Toc Travel again.

Lewton Wen was waiting for him. "Can he hear me now?" Lewton asked.

Rejoyce held a scanning device spinning aerials. "Yes…He's with us now."

"Fine," said Lewton. "Baum, you there?"

Gilead was floating, feet just off the ground. "Yes."

Lewton Wen began, "I've been told I was a bit tactless with you in our last dream visit. If I had my way, I'd get you back here right now. I wouldn't mess around a minute more. I'd go there myself and truss Gordon Mono up and haul him—okay, okay…sorry." He acknowledged the hands that had gone around his arm. "I get a little steamed thinking about it."

A woman stepped around Lewton. The sun of

the future shined on her glasses. She explained, "We want you to know we're all looking forward to you finding Gordon Mono. We know it's been difficult. We want to help your chances. How many times have you read your poem?"

"I don't know. I haven't been counting."

"Oh Nertz!" Wen bellowed.

The woman ignored that disruption. "We were afraid of that. You need new material. Don't worry, we have something. The computer generated a new poem for you." She read from a slip of paper:

"The lunch box.
 A long cube of sustenance.
We all take one.
We're all going to eat."

She looked up from the poem, regarding Gilead, "Don't look so surprised."

"It's fantastic!" Gilead cried. He saw himself in another dream, he was reading his brand-new poem into a sunflower-sized microphone, a hall full of people, a room as big as a church, and Gordon Mono sat in the front row applauding. The *Herald* hailed it a triumph, "A Poetry Event."

"Mr. Baum! Come back! We're not done yet. We need your assurance. This piece of paper won't make it to the other side where you are." She handed him the poem. "You've got to memorize it before you wake. Concentrate with all your might. Can you remember it, Gilead? When you're awake, you'll need to write it down immediately, before it fades."

"I'll remember it," he promised. The toes of his shoes lightly brushed the paving, one foot went right through. With all the intensity he could muster, Gilead studied the poem, read it and repeated the words. While the dream connection fell apart like sand.

It was six o'clock. Gilead woke up as if the alarm went off. It didn't need to—going to work every day he had grown used to waking up at this hour. He stretched an arm from the blanket and turned on the bedside lamp. His record leaned in the 50-watt light. Oh yes…Finally, he could listen to it.

Morning is what he'd been waiting for since last night. Sleep was just an ocean in between. He put on a bathrobe, grabbed the record and left his room. The telephone in the hall was asleep, he hoped everyone else in the house was too.

Try as he might to be quiet, the wooden stairway groaned and squeaked under his weight. The Wallace Stevens Poetry House was brittle. He wanted to descend as a shadow would.

The first clue that he wasn't alone was the smell of burnt toast. Then, as he got closer to the ground floor, he heard the TV.

Puppets were making a commotion. He stopped on the stairs, stopped upon a creak. Someone was watching *Kukla, Fran and Ollie*. The house was awake, the turntable was out of his reach, guarded by the clacking jaws of a dragon. Gilead shut his eyes. Why? Would he ever get to hear the record? It made him question his fate in 1955.

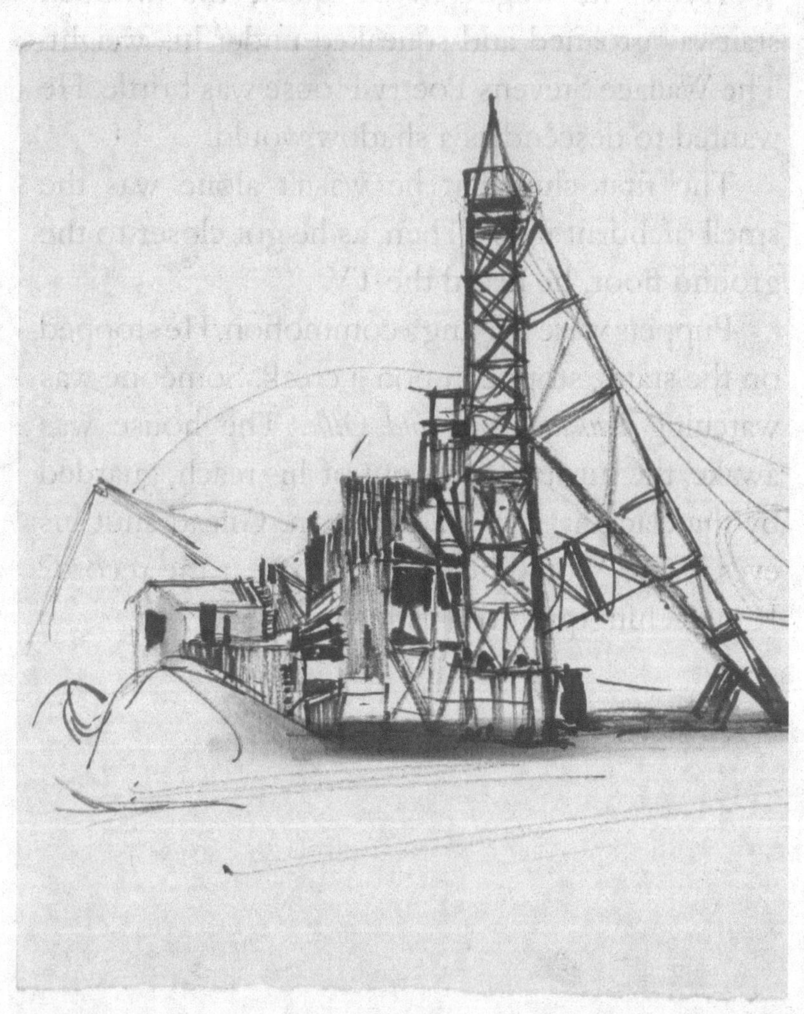

27

RADIO FREE AMERICA

Gilead Baum wasn't the only one carrying a record. Constance DuCanne set out that morning with hers. It was fun to drive the old Studebaker, though she had to keep a grip on the steering wheel and heave it around corners, plowing ahead, nothing like the winsome velocipedes of the future. When she turned onto Keene Street, she was nearly there. She drove past the house to check it out, to spot the black sedan of an FBI agent if one was there. Everything looked like a calm new day. She parked under a budding chestnut tree just around the next corner, out of sight of the house. It was the first week of spring, winter was still in the cold air, but the birds let you know those old days were numbered.

Hard to believe, a house colored like a lemon was a radio transmitter. The neighbors might have noticed a little more static than usual on *Captain Kangaroo* and close examination of the backyard would find something strange about the antenna wire running up the flagpole. Constance couldn't help thinking the yellow house was a pirate ship afloat on the green lawns and picket reefs.

Above the neighborhood an airplane made for the airport. The birds were singing. Her shoes clicked on the cement path. When she got to the house, she knocked eight raps, "La Marseillaise" played on a door. A purple finch trilled in the maple behind her. She wondered if she should have tried in back, she must look odd standing there, like someone selling invisible encyclopedias or vacuum cleaners door to door.

"Who is it?" a muffled voice riddled.

"It's the plumber," she replied, "I've come to fix the sink."

That was it, the correct answer, and the door swung open enough to let her in.

She was surprised. There was no sign of revolution. It was an ordinary living room, a couple couches, a TV set, a bookshelf, a still life painting on the wall. Quiet.

"This way," said the fellow beside her. Nothing unusual about him either, he could have been showing her the ropes at a department store on

Cornwall. He even wore a suit, but that wasn't unusual then. Constance too had arrived in 1955 looking to fit in, skirt, jacket, handbag. What they were doing couldn't be seen, it could only be felt, the rhythm, the lyrics, a song that could get in your head and change the way you think. When he opened the door for her at the end of the hall, she saw a turntable, a jumble of wires, a microphone. A slip in the window curtain revealed the backyard view of lawn, a picnic table, a redwood fence, trees and a roof on the other side. Electric wires strayed overhead. Aurora Avenue was a few blocks away. Some of those cars might be listening.

28.
MONTGOMERY WARD

In ten minutes, she was running. Away from the pirate antenna disguised as a house, away from the police on Keene Street, towards the avenue where she could get lost in the crowd. Constance was lucky the fellow in the Montgomery Ward suit distracted the police so she could escape. In her hurry, she left a record spinning, her others in a stack by the player, and all she had with her was Gilead Baum's. That was supposed to be the encore. If only she had time to play it—maybe his poem could have washed over this town and spread over the air far across this country until everyone felt the change. No more unhowled unheard wail in the night, it was time to wake up, go from one dream into another.

She didn't stop until she got to the J.C. Penney on Aurora. Her neck was sore from looking back, but she didn't see anyone chasing her and no sound of sirens, just people and cars and pigeons on the fire escape above her.

She looked over her shoulder one last time before she went in the store.

She was in Penney's for half an hour. Another day in 1955, going somewhere, wherever.

If there was an all-points bulletin squawking from police car radios, with agents placed on the corners smoking and watching for her, she was ready. She wasn't noticed as she left the store, wearing a yellow hooded jacket and checkered cigarette pants. Casual, she thought, be casual. She stopped at the Rexall and went inside to use a telephone.

Two blocks from her, a bus left the terminal. Gordon Mono looked out the window. For a moment in time he was frozen, looking out of the foggy glass. What a perfect cover that would be for his book.

29.
10th PLACE

After his disappointing visit downstairs, Gilead returned to his room and landed back on those rented noisome lopsided springs. To be drawn back and forth in such a fruitless endeavor, he thought, is this what the knights endured in search of the Holy Grail? He felt too tired to try anymore and he closed his eyes.

"Oh no…" He was at Tic Toc Travel, he had been tuned in and trapped again. Is this what dreams were like? Why were people so crazy to have them? He preferred the black sleep where nothing happened.

Gilead was familiar with the setting. The only difference was the time. Day was gone, it was night. And nobody else was around. Unless you counted the moths puttering around the neon rooftop sign. Or the bat that dipped after one and almost got it.

"Over here, Baum."

125

Gilead turned. The clipboard robot stood in a pool of flickering spotlight. It held the transmitter with the spinning aerials. "Where are the others?" Gilead asked.

"It's just you and me, pal."

"What's going on?"

The robot snickered, "You're having a dream, dummy. Now listen, time is short. I know you like being there in the past. I can make it so you stay there. I just need you to do something for me."

The dreamworld fluttered for a moment. In the Wallace Stevens Poetry House hallway, a phone was ringing.

The robot quickly continued, "In the trunk of your car, I hid seventeen grand. That's a lot of money for back then. I want you to bet it all on Red Rube to come in 10th place."

"Red Rube? Is that a horse?"

"That's right. It's a horse. And it's racing in the Grand National. You do that for me and I'll make sure you're done with the future for as long as you want. Listen, I'll even send you more poems—I got connections—if that sweetens the deal."

It did. If Giliad was going to be a poet, he needed to keep getting poems. What did it matter if it came from a robot in the future? Isn't that what inspiration was? Some strange message arriving out of the blue, aimed at someone who would notice. The telephone rang and rang and some distant part of Gilead wanted to go pick it up, but how could he if he was stuck in a dream?

"You got that?" the robot worked at the control box dials, pitching the aerials, "Red Rube is the horse, tenth place, there's cash in the Maverick trunk. Got it?"

Before he could say another word, Gilead opened his eyes. His room was dusty with sun. The sound in the hallway had stopped, he missed the call.

30.
ATOMIC PONGO

A voice growled in the darkness, "We live in a land of watercolor. Do you know this watery world? Others like you have come here, allowed to stay for a little while, or at least for as long as their dream lasts." Thunder rumbled. "One little drop of rain can start the world. And while rain clouds bring life, another cloud can end it." The black and white on the screen exploded and turned into a cloud of sparkling radiation drifting out of the desert. It hissed across the ground. "From outer space, looking in past the cloudy veil that covers this planet, a city in America looks much like any other city. You could drop to the ground in most any town on a rainy night when the streets are wet and a neon light burns like a matchstick on a building, above a door. Be a raindrop looking for somewhere to land. What about that girl opening the door? You don't need to stand outside in the cold, something is happening inside where it's warm." Music, conversation, a coffee machine steams and clacks like the metal wheels of a train on a track.

Hiding in the dark from the day at the Avalon matinee, Constance was watching *Atomic Pongo* for the second time. She knew how the story begins. A lock rattles off a circus train door and a gorilla leaps from the boxcar. It climbs into the trees overlooking the city nightlights. The leaves tremble in the wind. The twinkling atomic cloud approaches and rains on Pongo. The first time Constance saw that unraveled ape mask lean towards the town below, she figured she was in for another King Kong fable. But she was wrong. The creature has been given new life. It can speak its mind and its words are poetry. It was quite a ride, but for the second show, she knew how the story was going to end.

While the gorilla became the hit of the coffeehouse circuit and a song on the bongos began, Constance left her seat. She hurried up the aisle under the moonlit flow of the movie, pulling her yellow hood around her face.

"More popcorn, miss?" said the girl at the counter.

"No thanks." Constance headed for the phonebooth but there was one more question called after her.

"What do you think of the movie, miss? You must like it!"

Constance spun her finger next to her head. In the future that meant extraordinary. In 1955 it was the sign for crazy.

The girl laughed.

Constance kept a pocketful of coins for jukeboxes and telephones. She swung the wooden phonebooth door open, folded herself into a small narrow room with a window and got a dime. She was relieved to hear Gilead after a couple rings.

She explained what happened and she would have said more, but he hushed her. They couldn't afford to get in trouble with the cops. He imagined an agent listening to them, wired into a switchboard, a smoking ashtray near at hand. "We can't talk on the phone," Gilead said, "Meet me…let's see, meet me at the place you called me Galahad."

"Oh…" She placed a hand to her hair.

"Remember? Where you ran up to my car and I asked you about my poem and you said you had enough to make the record."

"Oh, right. Yes, we could meet there. That's not too far to walk."

"What about your car?"

She thought of her Studebaker, around the corner from Keene. Too bad Tic Toc Travel had given her such a conspicuous car. "I'm afraid to go back for it." It wouldn't matter if she did, the car was already gone. "But I need it." She wanted to explain, if she could get to her car she could return to the future, emptyhanded yes, but at least not doing time.

He said, "We must wait until dark. Meet me in our place. How about eight o'clock?" We need to discuss our future, he wanted to say.

"I don't know how many more times I can watch this movie."

"Just stay safe."

"I will," she promised.

<h1 style="text-align:center">31.
RED RUBE</h1>

For some reason the name Red Rube was on Gilead's mind. He started the Maverick and pulled into the street and headed for downtown, where the mill castled on the shore and there were buildings huddled around it, with neon signs crowding the streets. "Red Rube," he said aloud. What did it mean? Why was it vexing him? He repeated the name again and again, running it like an engine in the back of his mind while he drove.

Going past the Avalon, Gilead noticed the two words on the marquee, *Atomic Pongo*, but they couldn't distract him from his chant. At the next stoplight, he realized the car was driving itself, the steering wheel slid smoothly between his hands. While he was preoccupied with "Red Rube, Red Rube" the car was making its way steadily to where it wanted to be. A storefront was boarded up, a brick building offered rooms by the night. This was the part of town where night was always waiting in the wings. A pool hall, a bar. The brake pedal pushed, the wheel jumped against his hands and the Maverick veered into a spot against the curb in front of Louie's Betting Shop.

Now he knew. Red Rube was a horse. The Grand National. Bet on him. Then, like a photograph in his mind, he saw $17,000 dollars in a little tin box in the trunk. He left the car and went around to the bumper. He keyed the latch open and the box was right where he thought it would be. Like the car driving itself, his arm seemed to move on its own, as it reached forward and tucked the box into his suit coat. "Red Rube," he whispered and shut the trunk.

Cigarettes were crushed on the pavement, left in the same dead way the tide rolls from the broken shells on the shore. Gilead knew what he was getting himself into, he'd seen enough movies from the 1950s to know that film noir was still around. And sure enough, when he pushed the door open and went in, the first person he met was an Elisha Cook Jr. lookalike.

Gilead told him, "I want to see Louie."

"There is no Louie." The beady eyes glinted. "He don't exist. If you got something to say, say it to me."

"Okay then, okay, I will. I want to make a bet. I want seventeen grand on Red Rube. Grand National." Gilead felt elated for saying that, as if he had broken through a wall holding him back.

"Red Rube?" the man raised an eyebrow, tipping his fedora. His yellow teeth formed a grin, "You kidding me? Seventeen Gs on that nag?"

Gilead placed the tin box on the counter and pushed a dish of toothpicks aside. He opened the lid and revealed the stack of bills. He repeated, "Seventeen thousand on Red Rube to win."

The man who looked like he was poisoned in *The Big Sleep* put a hand over the box and hunched forward. A blues was running the jukebox in the corner. He said, "I'll get you a ticket."

32.
LEAVING *the* AVALON

Was it her fourth time watching the movie? Was she still able to count? Constance had grown so accustomed to the film it could have been the wallpaper in her room. Like a tapestry, the story began with the circus train by her door, and wrapped past the Bohemian cafés and the radiator, carried under the window, slept in her bed, across another wall filled with poetry, to end with the Nobel Prize, stopping back at the door. By now, the night was surely falling, and she felt pretty confident she was safe to leave the Avalon. That's why she nearly screamed when a cold hand touched her shoulder.

"Pardon me," said the man behind her seat. "Please, I don't mean to alarm you. My intentions are merely to thank you for the record."

"That's right…" she recognized the shadow, "You were at Shell's. I'm glad you liked it."

"It was," he paused, finding the right word,

"most hypnotic."

She wasn't sure if she liked his eyes. She admitted that she was just leaving, she saw the movie before, and he asked to accompany her, at least as far as the door. There was something he wanted to tell her. It was hard for her to imagine what that could be. Johnston Dracula was a mystery. He hobbled with her, up the aisle, through the red curtains into the lobby. The windows in front were dark. They stopped near the glass with the night spilling in and he told her, "Allow me to explain. Listening to your record…for the first time in a long time, I felt human again." His black eyes glittered in his waxy skin. "Believe me, I know the feeling of night, hunting and being hunted, I have been running from trouble for ten hundred years. You, my dear…" his weary theatrical voice hesitated, eyes pinched on her, "…are no stranger to trouble too?"

She found herself telling him the trouble she was in. It seemed absurd that playing songs on the radio could cause so much alarm—wasn't there room in the air for everyone?—and it was just as strange to be explaining it to a vampire. If that's what Johnston Dracula was. He certainly dressed the part.

"If you are worried about being seen, may I offer you my cape? Wear this and you will be protected. You will be nothing but a shadow as you pass through their world."

For a moment, she considered. She wondered what that would be like to be invisible on the sidewalk, to cast no reflection on the windows she passed. No, it seemed too much like being a ghost. She politely declined, telling him she would take her chances the same way she always did.

He bowed his head.

Then she suddenly asked, "So why can I see you when you're wearing your cape?"

His coal black eyes twinkled again. "Not everyone has your gift."

33.

The EVENING EDITION

Gilead Baum clipped the betting ticket under the car's windshield visor and drove to The Crooked Stairs. The café wasn't far, it wasn't that big a town though it would be one day. Things come and go. In fifty years where there used to be cow fields and the Moonlite Drive-In, a mall will tempt away all the big marble stores from downtown, abandoned like Roman relics: the Woolworths, the Avalon, and the vanished last cable car. Gilead decided it must have been a dream that told him to bet on a horse, where else could he have got that information? And all that money in the trunk of the car! Just like the poets say, some muse must have whispered in his ear.

It was hard to miss Constance DuCanne, wearing yellow like a tulip planted beside the café. And the Ford Maverick was obvious to her. She gave him a small wave.

The lampposts made phosphorus glows like

fishing lures in the sky. The dream-boxes had been removed from the heights.

"You've had quite a day today," he said as she quickly got in.

"You're telling me." She held her handbag on her lap. Gilead's record was all she carried, the only survivor from the raid on the pirate radio station. *The Herald Evening Edition* would go frontpage with the story.

Keene Street was nearing. So many branches stretched over the road, once it was summer they would make a solid green canopy. What was a quiet lemon-yellow house a day ago had turned into a crime scene. The lights were out, a blue lantern was left on the doorstep, there was a DO NOT ENTER sign nailed to the door. Two people were talking on the curbing, looky-loos by the look of them.

"Okay," said Constance, "Take a left ahead, it's coming up."

"I don't see any police," Gilead said. "Maybe it's a cold case now."

"Do you think my records are still inside?"

He shook his head, "They probably took them as evidence."

"Here's the street, go left."

The Maverick headlights shined down the sleepy street. Houses set back from the sidewalks. Their windows flickered with the moon colors of *The Ed Sullivan Show*.

Constance said, "Where's my car?"

Gilead braked, "Where'd you park?"

"Right there!" she tapped the window. "It's gone, look."

They rolled past a Studebaker-sized emptiness. They had no way of knowing it was carried back into the future, where it began in the Tic Toc Travel lot. Rejoyce reached into the car and turned off the blinking snowglobe and pocketed it. Then she told Lewton Wen the big news, that Constance wasn't inside.

34.

A HAUNTED CAR

"Remember that night when you joked that you're a time-traveler?"

He liked being with her and didn't easily forget. "The same night you called me Galahad."

Constance laughed, "You'll never let me live that down." As they passed Shell's, she turned to see if the jukebox was still working its spell. The windows were clouded with steam. Then she got right to the point, "I had to sign a form in triplicate that I'd never tell anyone what I am, but I have to tell you. I'm a time-traveler too."

At first he didn't know if she was joking. It took him until the next stop sign to turn to her. She was staring at him. Suddenly he remembered seeing her in a dream. They were at Tic Toc Travel. She was the one they were having trouble with, the same trouble they were having with him it turned out. They were both stuck in 1955, failing to find the same thing: Gordon Mono.

The car was driving itself again. Gilead figured it must be some update from the future. No drivers were needed anymore, everyone was a passenger, you were just swept along like a leaf. Gilead couldn't even pretend to be driving, it was obvious they were in a haunted car.

Constance said, "You would think we'd be a little scared by a car driving itself. Where do you think we're going?"

"I don't know. We'll find out when we stop."

"Or run out of gas. I wonder what mileage this clunker gets."

It took Gilead a week, but he had grown fond of the Ford Maverick and he was quick to defend it, "I don't know about that, this is considered a sensible driving option in 1973." They turned on Sunset Drive and he had an idea where the car was taking them. "We might as well enjoy the ride while it lasts."

The lights of the city were behind them, but something ahead of them, just over the next hill, was glowing like the flying saucer in *The Day the Earth Stood Still*.

35.

The MOONLITE DRIVE-IN

The car parked them along the back fence outside of the drive-in. It was familiar territory, very near to where Gilead landed in 1955. There weren't nightmare creatures from the sea on the screen tonight. The sign on the road read *East of Eden*. James Dean was still alive and he was thirty feet tall.

"Let's go lean on the fence and watch," Constance said.

"Sure." The car windows rolled down automatically. The radio came on. It was tuned to the signal transmitted from the aerial atop the snack shed. The Moonlite soundtrack didn't carry far, over the audience and the Maverick roof, out to the edge of Sunset. Cars going by could hear the movie for half a minute before it faded. James Dean was pouring his heart out, doomed as ever.

They crossed the grass, hopped a ditch to the old cow fence. The cows were all moved to the

146

other side of the street, this meadow was for movies.

Gilead pointed, "Right there is where I popped into this time."

"I've never been to a drive-in before," said Constance. "There's still a lot of things I haven't experienced here. This time is a whole other world and there are changes coming, you can tell. I'm excited to hear the music. I'd like to be a part of that. I feel like I already am, it feels like my work is only beginning."

Gilead said, "I like being a poet." He knew there was more in him he wanted to say. He added, "In seven years there's a World's Fair in Seattle. I'd like to see that."

They watched the movie at the end of the field. The parked cars glimmered in rows, grown almost back to them.

"What do you think we should do?" Gilead asked her.

She didn't have an answer, she had been thinking about that question for days.

"I bet on a horse," he admitted and then before she could respond, there was a pop like a balloon. They both turned around. The car was gone into thin air.

It appeared instantly in the future where Rejoyce was waiting. She opened the door and removed the blinking snowglobe and shut it off. She looked over the rooftop at Lewton Wen. She didn't have to say anything, her face said it all. The cars were back, but their drivers were lost in 1955.

James Dean jumped off a train, landing on the gravel.

Rejoyce picked up the handbag left on the car's bucket seat.

With no more sound for Gilead and Constance, the movie was all about changing colors. You had to make your own version of reality for what was happening. Stars were shining overhead. The Milky Way Galaxy.

Rejoyce yelled, "I found the record! They did it!"

Constance groaned, "Oh no! I left my handbag in the car."

Gilead stared at the bare roadside, "There goes my betting slip too. So much for my life as a millionaire."

"Gilead! Your record was in my handbag. What will they think?"

Good question. Gilead and Constance would never know.

In the future, Lewton's team went right to work. They understood it was not Gordon Mono to salvage their dreams. Why would it be someone who left nary a trace? Did he even exist at all? There was only hearsay, the word of two buzzy time-travelers who said they'd seen him. Buzzy? No, Constance and Gilead were heroes! They sacrificed themselves to send their precious record artifact forward in time where it could break the curse. The *Herald* ran with the story and included the recording, DRS #28, in each issue sold. The sides were played from the town's air raid speakers, in the telephone wires, and for 24 hours every radio and television station beamed to anywhere someone might be sleeping. Even the bridge underpass. "Transit" and "Going Somewhere" repeated over roofs and echoed down the long brick alleys, passed along from car to car, and when picked up by the wind on the airwaves that night, dreams reached far away as California.

36.
WHO IS SUSAN DELFIN?

"Ashtabula is beautiful this time of year, but this isn't Ashtabula. Here it's cold, raining off and on, windy and gray. Tomorrow is today." The audience at The Green Marilyn clapped appreciatively. He was right, it wasn't Ashtabula, which sounded like a tropical Shangri-la, this was still winter in their Northwest factory town and spring had to be slowly reeled in like a kite, fought like a fish deep in another world. An autoharp played while he went back to his table and the next poet stood up and made her way to read.

Susan Delfin held a little square of homemade paper, soft as a kitten's ear. She sat on the chair by the lamp and waited for the song to end, then she said, "This is a new poem, written in the manner of Gilead Baum." He hadn't been around for very long, but his mantra made a ripple in the pond. Her voice carried into the room:

"The sugarbowl. A deep cup of sweet
We all dig in
We're all stirring tea."

Her sincere imitation was a thing with feathers that flew from her hands and drafted in the applause carrying it in the air around the room until it came back to perch on Susan Delfin. Quiet as a mouse she returned to her chair and put on her coat while the autoharp spidered and she left the café without delay. She was shy about poetry. She wouldn't organize a Gilead Baum Night at the Marilyn, with candles and a reporter from the *Herald*, but she wasn't done celebrating him.

Once spring rolled around, she began her biggest tribute, tall enough to need a ladder and three cans of paint. She lived in an apartment on Indian Street. It had the lost color of a pressed flower. In the 1950s it already felt old, slightly tilted and slumped, with a wooden stairway outside that poked like crooked bones up the back to the third floor. In the alley behind, there was a doomed car, weeds, garbage cans, bamboo, and some fresh dandelions dripped like the path of a gondolier.

She leaned out from the rickety rail with a

brush, painting his poem on that hidden side of her apartment building.

You have to know the alleys of town to see that writing, you had to be poor, carefree or purposeless, you had to avoid the streets and wander on foot with the puddles, mud and blackberry. Junk cemeteries, graveyards of rust and clutter and the litter of rented rooms, gloom and sunlight, wind and rain, where cats and crows watch you go.

Picture all the old alleys that run across blocks. In the rainy winter and early spring there's often a stream on either side. Seldom paved, usually dirt or gravel, these are timeless channels to and fro. What used to be can still be. A goat, a tin car, a ghost or two. You could carry a giant ball of twine and go back and forth on them for miles, tying up town. A map of the tangles would lead you to where she used to live.

Near the end of the 20th Century, after all the changes, her apartment building is still there. As if to hide, it has pulled overgrowth in around it. An untidy scrabble of juniper, hollies, ferns, moss and ivy, stones and sparrows, laurels and some broken bottles. The siding has turned sallow. The garbage cans are still there. A motorcycle broods on its kickstand. The stairway has been patched a hundred times. Stilted beams hold it up. A wooden home is like a boat, in or out of the water it can't last forever, it always needs repair. Three lines of fading letters are spelled on the wall. Someone needs to repaint them before they wear away. If Gilead Baum was to mean anything, it was because of his words.

THE END

Robert Kuch 56'

Way up yonder above the sky
A bluebird lived in a jaybird's eye
Buckeye Jim, you can't go
Go weave and spin, you can't go
Buckeye Jim

Way up yonder above the moon
A blue jay nest in a silver spoon
Buckeye Jim, you can't go
Go weave and spin, you can't go
Buckeye Jim

—Burl Ives

AFTERWORD
the book's dream

For every novel there are scenes that never make it into the finished work. They scatter the floor like cut strips of film. As usual I find them hard to throw away, so I collected them and strung them together to give you a look. They almost tell the same story, not quite, as if this is the dream of our book.

Back in the day, he would read his poetry all around the city. There were coffeehouses, cellar shops and cafés.

Works in the Dream Deposit. Processes the dreams of people in town.

Set in 1952, a government study catching dreams in their town, sci-fi streetlights with receivers to measure the sky.

Gilead never noticed the lamppost receivers. It's hard to believe people used to throw their dreams away. Now we know better, there's so much to be gained from them. I do wonder about all those other lives and what was lost.

Will he watch his own dream that he had during the day? On the Leopold roof he ties his poems to the pigeons, they end up with breadcrumbs at the park bench where a girl is collecting them.

Constance has also gone back in time, to record a little town in 1955. The paper mill, the trains, the side streets when they wake in the morning.

He comes out of The Crooked Stairs and something takes him back to the start of the book.

The clipboard robot asks, "Have you got anything we can use? Did he say anything that might help? Anything at all?"

"Oh, sure, that's right, he gave me something." Gilead digs into his pocket. "Here, I brought you a poem from the past."

The robot's eye glowed. Obviously, it was thinking this is the poem they've all been looking for! Then it read it out loud, "Pete and Repeat were on a boat. Pete fell out, who was left on the boat?" The robot paused. "What's that mean? This is a poem?"

"Do you know the answer?"

"Of course. Repeat." Then the robot shuddered. It had to rewind and say it again, "Pete and Repeat were on a boat. Pete fell out, who was left on the boat?" Then it said, "Repeat," and the same thing happened again and again.

"You can't stop, can you?" she asked. The robot repeats endlessly, has to be unplugged and dragged off.

Like crabtraps flown up into the sky to catch dreams. He's only supposed to catalog the dreams, but he goes into hers.

There are people I only know in dreams I never meet in real life. Except for her.

    She asks for his phone number.
    "77," he answers.
    "What?"
    "I'm 112 years old."

She tells him, "I'm sorry, I have to go, I'm on the run from the police."

Johnston Dracula stands in the deep shadows gathered for night.

Phil Cook, needle and thread.

Her operator voice on the phone, "Time and temperature. 3:37 A.M. 33 degrees. I'm sorry that's all I'm able to say."

A candle in a jam jar burned on the street corner. He carried it home and set it by his bed at dawn, it was still burning twelve hours later when he woke in the winter dark.

Iron ore ray

"There are other time-travelers all the time, you're just not supposed to let on. We have to stay anonymous."

"How do you know there are?" She looked around the grocery. "Do you see others?"

Gilead paused and examined the aisle. "Not yet…I'll tell you when I do."

Supermarket green trading stamps

The Daily Tripe coffee house. A poetry reading hosted by Androcles Perm. He's the kind of guy it's easier to like when you're not in same room as him.

Lewis Windshield, café performer mime

In the library stacks, a lean figure holding a book up close to his eyes.

There was a rumor they kept artists locked in a room upstairs and forced them to paint masterpieces of despair which they sold to museums and auction houses. It's just a rumor.

He remembers the dream where he got another poem. He contacts the future by shortwave radio in his car and his call is directed to Poetry. He requests another poem. "I wrote a new one," Gilead tells her later.

"No!" She is genuinely surprised.

That second poem was in him somewhere planted by a dream, and if he was able to catch it, there must be more that could be reached.

She made a garden in the lot. A flower seed packet she bought at Safeway.

He walks into puddles.
Meets Susan the mermaid.

Chicken coop in the rain. The chicken is reluctant to go down the ramp into its pen.

Discovers a letter about the Sleep Bomb they're going to drop that will trap everyone into sleep forever.

His reality is between reality and dreams.

He dreams about being a highschooler, listening
to a radio show, *Son of the Wolfman*, 1950s songs.

You know you're in a dream when it's not night
anymore, the weather has changed, also it might not
be the same town or if it is, there are differences.

There are three times set on the car dial:
1952, 1972, 2023

Gilead drives the Ford back in time to 1952 to save Gordon's book of poetry. They need to stop him from burning it.

If it wasn't for her, he might have become a shadow. Constance gets him a radio commercial, uses his voice to sell detergent.

His poetry was coming to life again in the newspaper, radio, written on her apartment building.

Drives car to repair shop to get windshield repaired.

A mistake is made, someone wasn't paying attention and the replaced window doesn't work right. Like a wide movie screen, it shows him a different town, thousands of miles away, the view of a street in Concord, Massachusetts.

Mechanic explains, "That happens sometimes with older cars."

Gilead replies, "This car is from the future!"

"That's what you say."

"It's true!"

"Okay. Settle down." The mechanic shook his head. He didn't want to get into it. How could the future create an automobile like this? What happened to America? What happened to Cadillac and the Thunderbird?

Car takes Gilead to 1973, its home, telling him, "This is where I belong."

He leaves it there on his further way to the future.

The only thing to counteract the effect of the lingering radiation is a poem.

The future was another realm—it was like thinking about Heaven—he knew it was there, he knew things were going on there and he knew they were keeping an eye on him.

AMERICAN MANTRA
Writing:
October 31—April 3, 2023

From *The Robert Huck Museum* (2022)

Books by Good Deed Rain

Saint Lemonade, Allen Frost, 2014. Two novels illustrated by the author in the manner of the old Big Little Books.

Playground, Allen Frost, 2014. Poems collected from seven years of chapbooks.

Roosevelt, Allen Frost, 2015. A Pacific Northwest novel set in July, 1942, when a boy and a girl search for a missing elephant. Illustrated throughout by Fred Sodt.

5 Novels, Allen Frost, 2015. Novels written over five years, featuring circus giants, clockwork animals, detectives and time travelers.

The Sylvan Moore Show, Allen Frost, 2015. A short story omnibus of 193 stories written over 30 years.

Town in a Cloud, Allen Frost, 2015. A three-part book of poetry, written during the Bellingham rainy seasons of fall, winter, and spring.

A Flutter of Birds Passing Through Heaven: A Tribute to Robert Sund, 2016. Edited by Allen Frost and Paul Piper. The story of a legendary Ish River poet & artist.

At the Edge of America, Allen Frost, 2016. Two novels in one book blend time travel in a mythical poetic America.

Lake Erie Submarine, Allen Frost, 2016. A two week vacation in Ohio inspired these poems, illustrated by the author.

and Light, Paul Piper, 2016. Poetry written over three years. Illustrated with watercolors by Penny Piper.

The Book of Ticks, Allen Frost, 2017. A giant collection of 8 mysterious adventures featuring Phil Ticks. Illustrated throughout by Aaron Gunderson.

I Can Only Imagine, Allen Frost, 2017. Five adventures of love and heartbreak dreamed in an imaginary world. Cover & color illustrations by Annabelle Barrett.

The Orphanage of Abandoned Teenagers, Allen Frost, 2017. A fictional guide for teens and their parents. Illustrated by the author.

In the Valley of Mystic Light: An Oral History of the Skagit Valley Arts Scene, 2017. A comprehensive illustrated tribute. Edited by Claire Swedberg & Rita Hupy.

Different Planet, Allen Frost, 2017. Four science fiction adventures: reincarnation, robots, talking animals, outer space and clones. Illustrated by Laura Vasyutynska.

Go with the Flow: A Tribute to Clyde Sanborn, 2018. Edited by Allen Frost. The life and art of a timeless river poet. In beautiful living color!

Homeless Sutra, Allen Frost, 2018. Four stories: Sylvan Moore, a flying monk, a water salesman, and a guardian rabbit.

The Lake Walker, Allen Frost 2018. A little novel set in black and white like one of those old European movies about death and life.

A Hundred Dreams Ago, Allen Frost, 2018. A winter book of poetry and prose. Illustrated by Aaron Gunderson.

Almost Animals, Allen Frost, 2018. A collection of linked stories, thinking about what makes us animals.

The Robotic Age, Allen Frost, 2018. A vaudeville magician and his faithful robot track down ghosts. Illustrated throughout by Aaron Gunderson.

Kennedy, Allen Frost, 2018. This sequel to *Roosevelt* is a coming-of-age fable set during two weeks in 1962 in a mythical Kennedyland. Illustrated throughout by Fred Sodt.

Fable, Allen Frost, 2018. There's something going on in this country and I can best relate it in fable: the parable of the rabbits, a bedtime story, and the diary of our trip to Ohio.

Elbows & Knees: Essays & Plays, Allen Frost, 2018. A thrilling collection of writing about some of my favorite subjects, from B-movies to Brautigan.

The Last Paper Stars, Allen Frost 2019. A trip back in time to the 20 year old mind of Frankenstein, and two other worlds of the future.

Walt Amherst is Awake, Allen Frost, 2019. The dreamlife of an office worker. Illustrated throughout by Aaron Gunderson.

When You Smile You Let in Light, Allen Frost, 2019. An atomic love story written by a 23 year old.

Pinocchio in America, Allen Frost, 2019. After 82 years buried underground, Pinocchio returns to life behind a car repair shop in America.

Taking Her Sides on Immortality, Robert Huff, 2019. The long awaited poetry collection from a local, nationally renowned master of words.

Florida, Allen Frost, 2019. Three days in Florida turned into a book of sunshine inspired stories.

Blue Anthem Wailing, Allen Frost, 2019. My first novel written in college is an apocalyptic, Old Testament race through American shadows while Amelia Earhart flies overhead.

The Welfare Office, Allen Frost, 2019. The animals go in and out of the office, leaving these stories as footprints.

Island Air, Allen Frost, 2019. A detective novel featuring haiku, a lost library book and streetsongs.

Imaginary Someone, Allen Frost, 2020. A fictional memoir featuring 45 years of inspirations and obstacles in the life of a writer.

Violet of the Silent Movies, Allen Frost, 2020. A collection of starry-eyed short story poems, illustrated by the author.

The Tin Can Telephone, Allen Frost, 2020. A childhood memory novel set in 1975 Seattle, illustrated by author.

Heaven Crayon, Allen Frost, 2020. How the author's first book *Ohio Trio* would look if printed as a Big Little Book. Illustrated by the author.

Old Salt, Allen Frost, 2020. Authors of a fake novel get chased by tigers. Illustrations by the author.

A Field of Cabbages, Allen Frost, 2020. The sequel to *The Robotic Age* finds our heroes in a race against time to save Sunny Jim's ghost. Illustrated by Aaron Gunderson.

River Road, Allen Frost, 2020. A paperboy delivers the news to a ghost town. Illustrated by the author.

The Puttering Marvel, Allen Frost, 2021. Eleven short stories with illustrations by the author.

Something Bright, Allen Frost, 2021. 106 short story poems walking with you from winter into spring. Illustrated by the author.

The Trillium Witch, Allen Frost, 2021. A detective novel about witches in the Pacific Northwest rain. Illustrated by the author.

Cosmonaut, Allen Frost, 2021. Yuri Gagarin's rocket lands in America. Midnight jazz, folk music, mystery and sorcery. Illustrated by the author.

Thriftstore Madonna, Allen Frost, 2021. 124 summer story poems. Illustrated by the author.

Half a Giraffe, Allen Frost, 2021. A magical novel about a counterfeiter and his unusual, beloved pet. Illustrated by the author.

Lexington Brown & The Pond Projector, Allen Frost, 2022. An underwater invention takes three friends through time. Illustrated by Aaron Gunderson.

The Robert Huck Museum, Allen Frost, 2022. The artist's life story told in photographs, woodcuts, paintings, prints and drawings.

Mrs. Magnusson & Friends, Allen Frost, 2022. A collection of 13 stories featuring mystery and ginkgo leaves.

Magic Island, Allen Frost, 2022. There's a memory machine in this magical novel that takes us to college.

A Red Leaf Boat, Allen Frost, 2022. Inspired by Japan, this book of 142 poems is the result of walking in autumn.

Forest & Field, Allen Frost, 2022. 117 forest and field recordings made during the summer months, ending with a lullaby.

The Wires and Circuits of Earth, Allen Frost, 2022. 11 stories from a train station pulp magazine.

The Air Over Paris, Allen Frost, 2023. This novel reveals the truth about semi-sentient speedbumps from Mars.

Neptunalia, Allen Frost, 2023. A movie-novel for Neptune, featuring mystery in a Counterfeit Reality machine. Illustrated by Aaron Gunderson.

The Worrys, Allen Frost, 2023. A family of weasels look for a better life and get it. Illustrated by Tai Vugia.

American Mantra, Allen Frost, 2023. The future needs poetry to sleep at night. Only one man and one woman can save the world. Illustrated by Robert Huck.

Books by Bottom Dog Press

Ohio Trio, Allen Frost, 2001. Three short novels written in magic fields and small towns of Ohio. Reprinted as *Heaven Crayon* in 2020.

Bowl of Water, Allen Frost, 2004. Poetry. From the glass factory to when you wake up.

Another Life, Allen Frost, 2007. Poetry. From the last Ohio morning to the early bird.

Home Recordings, Allen Frost, 2009. Poetry. Dream machinery, filming Caruso, benign time travel.

The Mermaid Translation, Allen Frost, 2010. A bathysphere novel with Philip Marlowe.

Selected Correspondence of Kenneth Patchen, Edited by Larry Smith and Allen Frost, 2012. Amazing artist letters.

The Wonderful Stupid Man, Allen Frost, 2012. Short stories go from Aristotle's first car to the $500 dollar fool.

14 DAY BOOK

**This book is due on or before
the latest date stamped below**